I0744575

SOONER OR LATER

FROM THIS DAY FORWARD
BOOK 2

DARA GIRARD

ISBN: 978-1-949764727

Sooner or Later

Copyright © 2023 by Sade Odubiyi

Published by ILORI Press Books

Cover Design and Layout Copyright © 2023 ILORI Press Books

Cover design by ILORI Press Books

Cover Photo © Elet_1/depositphotos

All rights reserved. The reproduction, transmission or utilization of this work in whole or in part in any form by any electronic, mechanical or other means, now known or hereafter invented, including xerography, photocopying and recording, or in any information storage or retrieval system, is forbidden without written permission.

This is a work of fiction. Names, characters, places and incidents are either the product of the author's imagination or are used fictitiously, and any resemblance to actual persons, living or dead is entirely coincidental.

ILORI PRESS BOOKS, LLC

P.O. Box 10332

Silver Spring, MD 20914

www.iloripressbooks.com

BOOKS BY DARA GIRARD

Duvall Sisters

The Glass Slipper Project

Taming Mariella

A Reluctant Hero

The Black Stockings Society

Power Play

A Gentleman's Offer

Body Chemistry

Round the Clock

Return of the Black Stockings Society

Playing for Keeps

After Hours

A Private Affair

Just One Look

Private Lessons

The Main Attraction

Ladies of the Pen

Words of Seduction

Pages of Passion

Beneath the Covers

Henson Series

Table for Two

The Daughters of Winston Barnett

Remember My Name

Illusive Flame

Winterwood Lane

Promise Me

This Changes Everything

Sparks

Piece of Cake

Best Laid Plans

Her Tender Touch

Dream of Me

1

———

THE WEAPON WAS READY.

The target in sight.

Ava Kayode felt as if she were in the middle of one of the Spaghetti Westerns her great-grandfather used to like. Except this time the adversaries didn't face each other. One even had their back turned.

But it was still a showdown.

To Ava's left stood her older sister, Gwen, dressed in a beautiful beaded white wedding dress, the spring sun warming the steps of the concrete stairs of the church and, as if on cue, highlighting her brown skin, masterfully applied makeup, and artistically arranged black hair. No one would see her as dangerous.

That was her power. Her gift. But Ava held her breath as she saw Gwen grip the bouquet in her hands and a soft smile touch her full lips.

Ava shifted her gaze to Gwen's rival: The target.

Ava's half-sister, Maya, had always been an easy target.

Ever since she'd come to live with them as a fourteen year old after her grandmother had died, she'd been deemed the outsider. The result of a relationship their mother refused to discuss, Maya was a short, chubby little firecracker of a woman who most people didn't understand. A flower hating, rule breaking (she didn't even try to get the richly laced, golden and red colored *aso ebi* that Gwen expected the family to wear to the wedding. Instead choosing an ankhara styled dress, in the same color scheme, an outfit she'd worn to a recent naming ceremony, a definite 'no-no' in their Nigerian-American community) unemployed, single woman dangerously close to middle age at thirty-seven, and two years older than Gwen.

Their mother despaired of her ever being anything more than a constant disappointment. But there was still a lingering hope that her acceptably pretty face would encourage someone —anyone!— to take her off their hands. As if Maya were a used car they wanted to shift and not someone who had been supporting herself since she'd been driven out of the family house at nineteen only to return recently due to unfortunate circumstances.

Ava noticed the defiant look on Maya's face and the equally proud, arrogant grin on Gwen's face and knew the day was headed for disaster.

To the exquisitely dressed onlookers, standing tall with their heads covered in bright geles and caps, the bouquet toss was a show of sisterly optimism, on Gwen's part, that poor Maya's life wasn't the complete mess that everyone deemed it to be.

But Ava knew Maya and Maya didn't believe in superstitious optimism. She wasn't going to have it.

When Gwen tossed the bouquet in the air, Ava wanted to cry out, terror gripping her heart as if the bouquet had turned into a grenade.

It was too late to stop her. She knew that throwing the bouquet was as an act to humiliate Maya. Ava had overheard Maya more than once beg Gwen not to toss the bouquet at her.

But Gwen always did what Gwen wanted to.

Today would be no different.

Ava closed her eyes. She didn't want to see what would happen next. She gripped her hands together and silently prayed that Maya would do something uncharacteristic and follow the rules.

Please just catch the bouquet, Ava silently begged her. *I know you'll hate it. I know you hate flowers. I know Gwen's being a jerk, but please, just this once, please catch it. Please catch it.*

If Maya caught the bouquet, accepted the humiliation that came with it, then all would be well.

The collective gasp and the loud squeal of tires were the first ominous sounds of impending doom.

Then she heard the thud.

Ava gripped her hands tighter too afraid to open her eyes. She didn't want to face what had happened.

She felt people rushing past her and knew it wasn't good.

She slowly opened her eyes and saw the crowd racing to the parking lot.

"She tried to kill him," she heard one guest mutter.

Ava tried to politely make her way through the crowd, not bold enough to barrel her way through the way her younger sister Catherine, better known as Cat, was. But then Cat was as skinny as a reed and people barely noticed her so it was easy. Ava, although of similar medium height, wasn't as slenderly built, and her sweet features, caramel colored skin and the thirty year habit of pleasing others, made it hard to push her way through without apologizing for her existence if she unintentionally bumped into anyone. So it took her awhile to find a vantage point that allowed her to see what had happened.

But when she finally did...

She gasped and covered her mouth.

A man lay motionless on the ground.

Not just any man. An Adesina. They were a prominent, well respected family that had ties to the Kayodes that stretched back for centuries. This was bad.

Capulets and Montagues, Hatfields and McCoys or the Taira and the Minamoto bad, if not handled well. Family-tribe relationships were always a delicate balance.

Soon Maya's voice rose above the rest and started barking orders, which was no surprise, that's what she did well. Something she'd likely learned working with college students as a former art professor.

Ava saw Keeden grab Maya's wrist and say something to her. Ava took a deep breath, feeling her pulse slow. He was speaking. That was a good sign. Although the frown on Maya's face wasn't. Ava didn't doubt that Keeden would make her sister pay for whatever had happened.

The Kayodes would have to find a way to smooth this over.

Ava glanced at her sister, Cat, and gasped again. She raced over to her.

"What is wrong with you?" Ava said in a low whisper.

"Why?"

"You're smiling like you're enjoying this."

Cat shrugged unfazed. "I am."

"This is a disaster."

"Serves Gwen right."

"But poor Keeden. Stop smiling."

"No one notices me except you."

The statement was depressingly true. Born without classi-cally attractive features most people dismissed her. "Doesn't matter," Ava scolded. "Stop smiling. We're lucky his best friend Bryant isn't here. She would have been humiliated." Everyone knew their sister Maya had a big crush on him to Keeden's annoyance.

Cat schooled her features and said, "Might do them both good."

"You have a sick way of looking at things."

She wagged her finger. "Different. Not sick. And instead of worrying about me, you should worry about him." She nodded to something behind Ava.

Ava turned and saw her fiancé Folu Adeigbo standing motionless. If she didn't know he was human she would have thought he was a handsome statue. That a skilled artisan had taken dark oak and carved a man with a sharp jaw, tender lips and wide eyes.

Wide, terrified eyes.

"You'd better catch him before he faints," Cat murmured.

Ava spun back to her sister annoyed. "It was one time." Folu had been helping them clean out some boxes in the garage and a frog had jumped out of one of them. He had screamed and shoved Ava in front of him as if the little amphibian had turned into a man-eating crocodile.

It hadn't been a very good moment for either of them. Cat wouldn't let her forget it. "We all have our flaws. We're not all fearless like you."

"I'm hardly fearless," Cat said, "but I won't use you as a shield either. I know Dai wouldn't have."

The mention of her best friend almost made her laugh. If a frog had jumped out of a box, Dai would have probably caught it; made up a little victory dance, wiggling his wide shoulders, then taken a picture so he could show his son Donovan before letting the frog go. "Folu is not Dai."

"I know."

"He was hugging me for support."

Cat rolled her eyes. "He was hiding behind you like a—"

Ava held up her hand, stopping her words. "That's enough. Let me go check on him."

"Don't forget the smelling salts."

Ava pretended not to hear her sister's words as she hurried over to Folu. Cat was an anomaly. Everyone else liked Folu. He was attractive, smart, kind. People continued to applaud her at "the excellent catch" she'd made and she cared about him. He was a good man and she planned to raise a family and spend the rest of her life with him. She would not let her sister's criticisms let her not see all his good traits just because he had a couple of bad ones.

When Ava reached him she lightly touched his shoulder.

He jumped as if she'd administered an electric shock.

"Are you okay?" she asked, keeping her voice gentle.

He blinked quickly. "Did you see that?"

She made a noncommittal sound.

"It was awful."

"Yes."

He covered his eyes and shook his head. "Just awful."

"Yes." She didn't know what else to say. He looked devastated. "He'll be okay. At least he can move and speak and there are plenty of doctors and nurses to assess him."

"I'll never forget the sound of the thud." He started to shake.

She motioned to the church steps. "Come and sit down."

"I can't."

"At least let's head to the reception. We can..." Her words fell away when he shook his head again.

"I can't. I'm sorry. I'm too shaken to go and pretend..." His voice fell away and he hung his head. "I'm sorry."

Then he looked at her.

Unlike some, Ava didn't really believe in omens. But if she did, she would conclude that it was rarely a good omen when one's fiancé takes their hand and bursts into tears.

2

———————

"I'm sorry," Folu said, wiping his eyes with the back of his hand. "I don't think I can marry you. It wouldn't be fair."

They'd already been officially engaged for two years and didn't plan to marry for another two. If she were honest she'd admit she felt as if she'd been in a holding cell. Not quite a girlfriend or fiancée, but rather a handy accessory when it suited him. She'd been patient. She'd continue to be so. She'd dealt with his moments of panic before.

"Marriage is a long way off," Ava said gently. "We agreed to continue as we are right now."

He sniffed. "But it's not the future I want." He bit his lip. "When I saw Adesina on the ground my life flashed before my eyes. I imagined that it was me. What if I got hit by a car and I didn't make it? What would my regrets be? What are the things I wanted to do and didn't? I've been scared all my life and I don't want to be scared anymore."

"I understand. I won't stop you if you want to travel or move somewhere else, but we don't have to break off the engagement because of that. A relationship takes commitment and adjustment. I'll adjust."

He met her gaze. "The truth is I love you, but I don't want to marry you."

Ava took a deep breath determined to stay composed. "Are you actually dumping me at my sister's wedding?"

"I'm sorry."

"But why?"

He pointed at her. "Because of that."

She blinked. "What?"

"That look on your face. I find it terrifying."

"You just broke my heart and you call *me* terrifying?"

He nodded. "You should be angry or in tears or confused but you look so...serene. I don't know what you're thinking. I can't read you. To everyone else you're sweet and naïve and unassuming but to me..."

"To you...what?"

"You're stronger than I am and we both know it. I'm a weak man and you make me feel weaker. You make me feel ashamed of myself. Not because of anything you've done or said," he rushed to clarify. "But just because of who you are."

"Is what happened just an excuse?"

He frowned. "An excuse?"

"Did you meet someone else?"

"No," Folu said in a quiet voice filled with misery. "And part of me feels like I'm making a huge mistake by saying this to you. But another part of me feels relieved."

"I didn't know being with me has been so difficult," Ava said determined to keep her voice gentle and soothing. "I'm sorry you've suffered and not told me sooner." She covered his hand.

He pulled his hand away. "You're making it worse. Stop being so understanding. Tell me what you think. Slap me."

"We both know that won't solve anything. Our families are invested in this relationship too, remember?"

He sighed. "I know."

"We can't just do what we want without thinking about the consequences."

"Don't you feel suffocated sometimes? Don't you sometimes resent carrying the weight of your family's expectations?"

She'd never really allowed herself to think any other way. She felt honored that her parents had put so much faith in her. It gave her pleasure to make them happy. She didn't need to be a rule breaker like Maya. Toeing the line had worked so far. She'd never imagined it not working.

"Why don't we have a breather," she suggested. If she remained rational and reasonable, he'd see the folly of his ways. "Let's not make any rash decisions."

"I'm not marrying you, Ava. I can't give you what you need or deserve."

She prided herself on not being a violent woman. She didn't watch the bloody action movies her sister Cat couldn't get enough of. She never pictured herself physically hurting anyone.

But she knew there were other ways to administer pain.

Subtle, careful ways. Ways that would linger.

She may not believe in violence but she did believe in revenge. And at that moment, as she stared at Folu's red rimmed eyes, she thought of the years she'd devoted to him. The life she'd planned to have with him. The life he was taking away, suddenly she felt the burning, stirring need for revenge.

Of course she could force him to marry her. He was a weak man and she had learned how to manipulate him when necessary. Their engagement had been an idea she'd put into his head not something he'd thought of on his own.

He was trying to be defiant but she saw the fear in his eyes. With patience she could win him back.

She would be *very* patient.

But coming back to her, changing his mind, had to be his idea. She would have to play his silly game while making up her own rules.

Folu swallowed hard. "Please, Ava. Don't make this harder than it has to be."

"Okay."

"Really?"

The relief on his face almost made her laugh. "Yes," she said, hiding every hint of her anger. "How are we going to do this?"

Folu gave her a plan of action that she found ludicrous. No surprise, she did most of the planning for them.

They hadn't even gotten married yet but he had them divvying things up like they were in the middle of a divorce. "You take the blame and I'll take the pity."

Ava stared at him shocked. "No, I should get the pity and you get the blame. This is your idea, remember?"

"But you can handle it better than I can."

"It's easier for a man to have a broken engagement than a woman."

"Is there a way we could both get blamed?"

"You're the one who wants to do this," Ava said losing patience. "Why should I lie?"

"You know how it will look. No one will understand me leaving you. You have to leave me."

"But I don't want to."

Folu took her hand in his and she didn't pull away, even though for the first time he made her skin crawl. "You will thank me one day."

"Just not today."

He released her hand looking genuinely distraught. "I'm sorry."

She knew that he was and briefly—very briefly—she considered truly letting him go and not trying to win him back. But she knew this momentary panic couldn't replace years of planning and family expectations. "Give me time to think of what I can do. Until then don't mention our broken engagement to anyone."

"I won't."

She took a step forward, lowering her voice to a whisper. "Because if you do, you won't have a chance for your life to flash before your eyes. It will end faster than that."

He bit his lip and nodded his head then pointed at the parking lot. "Adesina's gone."

Ava turned and saw the crowd dispersing, the bright afternoon sun touching the golden accents on some of the pink, red or green colored geles and handbags. She noticed the faint scent of cigarette smoke and wondered where it was coming from. Cat motioned to her and pointed to herself, asking if she wanted her to stay, but Ava gestured for her to go, she'd talk to her later. Keeden had likely been sent to the hospital and the crisis had passed.

Her's was only beginning.

Revenge. As Ava marched to her car her mind filled with possible scenarios of revenge. But she knew winning Folu back was more prudent, sensible. It was what everyone would expect of her. It was what she expected of herself. She wasn't the brash and reckless type.

I love you, Ava. How come his words felt like a stab through the heart? He made her feel inherently unlovable. Revealing her true fear. That there was something about her that would keep happiness away. That everything about her was a façade.

That she truly was a fraud as much as she tried not to be. She was a good person and sweet and kind.

But yes... there was another darker side. She could be vain and competitive and a little mean. Nothing like Gwen, but she didn't like to be crossed.

Ava sat in her car and gripped the steering wheel until her fingers screamed in pain.

I know I can't give you what you need. Ava swore. How magnanimous of him. That was her biggest problem with him. Folu really was a nice guy. She could never really stay angry at him for long. Anger would have helped her think of ways to punish him. Instead she felt sad. She felt sad that she'd failed. He was confused. She had to figure out a way to win him back. That was all. The accident had shaken up a lot of people. But their chosen path was perfect. They blended well together.

She couldn't tell anyone. Most of her friends were somehow connected to the Nigerian-American community and one whiff of scandal would spread through with the fervor of an evangelist at a revival.

Of course his idea was ludicrous. Too much was riding on their marriage. She had to think of what to do to win him back. She would be strategic as she'd always been.

3

———————

"Where's Folu?"

Ava inwardly groaned as she watched people enjoying themselves in the large ballroom. Most guests were unaware of the debacle at the church since a large number of them only turned up for the reception, and for Gwen's sake, Ava was glad that the food flowed as well as did the laughter and good humor.

She hoped to protect her own mood but feared that would be a losing battle. She'd expected people to ask about her fiancé. She'd known the question would come but she'd still hoped to avoid it. Especially from Cat who sometimes looked nineteen instead of a decade older.

Ava glanced with awe and envy at the pile of delicious canapés stacked on her sister's plate. Cat could inhale ten buckets of Maryland blue crabs and not gain an ounce.

She schooled her features, making sure to keep her voice light, polite and neutral. "He wasn't feeling well," she lied. She and Folu had agreed it would be best if he went home feigning illness. She wasn't in the mood to pretend to still be a couple at her sister's reception.

Cat held out her plate. Ava shook her head.

Cat nodded then gestured to Maya and Gwen talking. Or rather Gwen (now dressed in the first of the three outfits she'd wear throughout the evening: A bright red gown that gave her the appearance of a high priestess that held the power and wrath to send a supplicant—Maya—to a doomed fate). "That conversation should be interesting. I'm surprised she showed up."

Ava looked at Maya in sympathy. "It wasn't her fault."

Cat sent her sister a knowing look. "Bet your eyes were closed when it happened."

"Only briefly."

"Right."

"I saw enough," Ava said defensive, "and I know Maya wouldn't hurt Keeden on purpose. At least not by getting him hit by a car," Ava quickly added.

"Gwen doesn't think so." Cat popped a canapé in her mouth and chewed slowly before she said, "What's the plan?"

"Plan?"

"Yes. When are you going?"

Ava frowned. "I don't know what you mean."

"No need to pretend you haven't been given orders."

She hadn't been given orders yet but they would come soon. She was the PR for the Kayodes, always ready to smooth things over. She would have to go to the hospital and speak of the family's embarrassment as a result of her sister's behavior.

"Mom hasn't said anything yet."

"She will."

She didn't. Her father did instead.

He found her when Ava was thinking of how to escape to

the ladies' room after the fifth person had asked her where Folu was. He'd caught her eye and motioned her forward.

She dutifully hurried over to him. He looked unusually grim, standing tall and rigid with the air of a military general facing the possibility of war.

"You know I hate asking this, but you're the only one I can trust to do what is necessary."

"You want me to go to the hospital."

He sighed relieved that she understood. "Yes. It's best that your mother and I keep a united front here, Gwen will be off to her honeymoon soon and Maya definitely can't go to the hospital after what she's already done." He looked over at Cat, munching on the end of a celery stalk, and briefly shivered in pity. "No one would want her offering words of comfort. It's akin to sending dead flowers."

Ava frowned at her father's criticism of Cat. "That's not fair."

"But it's true. She has other..." His voice faded away as he searched his mind. "...attributes. But you are our greatest prize. You'll be like bright sunshine. Will you go?"

"Yes. Of course," Ava said because she rarely said otherwise even at the moments she most wanted to. "But won't I be missed for the toast or the cutting of the cake?"

"I'll make excuses for you. Don't let your mother or sisters hear this, but addressing this issue is more important. Our family name is at stake." He squeezed her shoulder and looked at her as if he were sending a soldier off to battle. "I'm counting on you."

She nodded, resisting the urge to salute. "Understood."

His face relaxed into a smile. "Good."

After her father left, Cat sidled over to Ava's side like a sneaky crab. "So when are you going?"

"Soon."

"Want me to come with you?"

"I'd rather you go instead."

Cat's eyes widened with delight and mischief. "Really?"

"No, not really."

"I would behave myself."

"Dad asked me. Besides, I have to leave before they cut the cake."

Cat looked heartbroken that her sister would be denied such an event. "That's plain mean. It's a chocolate raspberry cake with—"

"I don't care."

"I'll save a slice for you." She held out her plate again. "At least have something to eat before you go."

"I don't have an appetite."

Cat narrowed her eyes. "Something's wrong."

"Nothing's wrong." Ava checked her watch. It was early, barely four o'clock, but she had no reason to stay. "I might as well get going now."

To her relief Cat didn't try to stop her.

4

———————

Laughter shouldn't be the first impulse when one walks into a hospital waiting room.

But the moment Ava stepped into the room and saw the Adesinas, she had to bite her lip to keep from giggling. Dressed in their elegant attire, they looked out of place in the crowded room—as conspicuous as fine china among floral paper plates.

Keeden's stepmother looked expectantly distraught. A bit too much so if Ava was to be honest. His father looked bored and annoyed as if a waiter had given him the wrong order. Clearly he saw his son's accident as an inconvenience.

Ava touched her hair to make sure it was still pinned in place. She'd taken off her gele and left it in her car so she wanted to make sure she still looked presentable. Certain she could approach the Adesinas without embarrassing herself (or shaming her family), she made her way through the crush of people, delicately holding her breath after passing a woman who smelled as if she'd taken a bath in bourbon and another who might not have taken a bath in years.

"You didn't have to come," Mr. Adesina said when he saw her.

Mrs. Adesina clasped her hands together in relief. "I'm so glad you did. This is awful," she said then shared a list of Keeden's injuries with such speed that Ava could only remember the words "broken" and "head." Or it could have been "hand." She wasn't sure and knew it best not to ask. She didn't want to appear as if she hadn't been listening and being suitably attentive. However, she found it difficult to keep an expression of concern since the Adesinas were seated and she was forced to stand because there were no other seats available. Her feet were starting to ache. Mr. Adesina made it clear he had no intention of giving up his seat and Mrs. Adesina was talking so much she probably didn't notice Ava's discomfort.

"He'll live," Mr. Adesina eventually said, cutting off his wife's words.

"We're so glad to hear that, Uncle," Ava said, using the customary respected address for someone older.

"But he's in pain," Mrs. Adesina said.

Mr. Adesina folded his arms. "Most of it likely in his head. He doesn't have a strong constitution."

"He keeps going on about an unfinished project and how he won't be able to finish because of his injury," Mrs. Adesina said to clarify.

"Dramatic as always."

"His work is important to him."

"But it's hardly critical. If he had the hands of a surgeon that would be different, but an artist?" Mr. Adesina sniffed in disgust.

Ava kept silent, used to Mr. Adesina's disinterest in his son's career. He took little pride in the world renown Keeden had managed to gain with his work. She knew it was best to change the subject.

"If there's anything you need—"

"We're fine," Mr. Adesina said before his wife could reply. "If we need anything we can ask Melody," he said referring to their daughter." Mrs. Adesina closed her mouth and nodded.

Ava quickly excused herself hoping she could escape before Melody arrived. In her rushed attempt she turned the corner and bumped into someone.

"Look where you're going!" the cocoa colored beauty said.

"I'm sorry."

Melody stopped and grinned. Not a pleasant expression. She shared her brother Keeden's good looks and slim build but not his kindness. And Keeden wasn't known for being particularly kind.

Ava inwardly groaned, hoping she would have missed seeing her. Melody had the cunning of a cat. She could see opportunity.

"So your sister nearly killed my brother," Melody said. "Are you trying to make sure we don't sue?"

"That won't happen."

"But it could."

Ava knew that Melody had also gotten the lecture of the centuries long relationship the Kayodes and Adesinas have had. A lawsuit wasn't going to come into play.

"Your family owns a business," Melody said. "There could be a financial upside to all this."

If anyone could start a war after years of peace and diplomacy it was Melody. But Ava wouldn't allow that.

"Your family is doing well too." An understatement. Mr. Adesina had a lucrative medical practice and Keeden was exceedingly wealthy.

"I saw Folu crying."

Ava silently groaned. Folu again! "He wasn't crying."

"He looked near tears."

"So? I'm surprised you noticed him at all considering what had happened to Keeden."

To her surprise the statement seemed to rattle Melody but she quickly regained her composure. "I happened to glance at him."

"I see."

"Is he alright?"

"You need to worry about your brother."

Melody made a dismissive gesture with her hand, looking as bored and unconcerned as her father. "Nothing could kill off Keeden that easily. He's fine. But I'm worried about you."

Melody never worried about anyone. Ava sighed. "What do you want?"

She looked shocked. "Nothing. I really was interested." She paused, with dramatic effect, before she said, "Of course I have been worried since *your* sister put *my* brother in the hospital. But what truly concerned me was seeing Folu crying."

Ava felt her heart constrict. "He was shocked after seeing what happened to Keeden."

"And then I heard something about him not wanting to get married."

She knew!! This awful woman *knew*. Maybe not everything, but enough.

Ava pulled out her wallet and held out a twenty dollar bill. "I'm fine. So is Folu."

Melody rested a hand on her chest, barely looking at the offered money. "But I'm still so very, very worried about you two."

Ava inwardly swore and pulled out another twenty. "You can stop."

Melody drummed her fingers unmoved. "I couldn't believe what I was hearing."

"And did you hear this while smoking a cigarette you'd

promised your parents you would quit?" she said, now knowing who'd been smoking nearby.

"I was stressed." Melody frowned and snatched the bills before Ava could take them back. "I guess we're even then," she said then stormed away.

Ava knew paying Melody to stay silent would only last so long. But it gave her enough time to plan what to do next. First she needed to get back to her car and take off her shoes, to let her pinched toes breathe. Her stomach grumbled. She now regretted not taking Cat up on her offer of food. She'd probably left the reception too early, but at least at the hospital she didn't have to worry about someone asking her where her conspicuously absent fiancé was.

Ava headed for the vending machines. To her relief this part of the hospital wasn't crowded. So she let herself limp her way down the hall to the row of machines.

She halted when she saw a shabby looking woman in a threadbare jacket and faded jeans, her brown hair pulled back into a haphazard ponytail, crying in front of one of the machines.

Ava cautiously approached her. "Are you alright?"

"It took my money and I can't get it to work," the woman said in a tearstained voice as if her world were coming to an end.

Ava looked and saw the chocolate covered potato chips stuck in the machine. "It's okay. I'll get it for you."

"You don't have to do that."

Ava put extra money in and when the two packages fell she handed them over to the woman.

"Keep one for yourself," the woman said.

Ava shook her head. "Not my kind of thing," she said then put more money in the slot and selected caramel covered popcorn.

"I can pay you back."

"No need." Ava lightly touched her arm. "Are you here with anyone?"

"No, it's just me." Tears streamed down her face. "This is so hard. I'm worried about my father."

Ava scanned the hallway then noticed a door that led out to a courtyard. "Come on. I think some fresh air might do you good." She led the woman to a bench near a row of purple and pink azalea bushes.

She touched her worn jacket, self-conscious. "I must look awful, but I was in the middle of spring cleaning when I got the call and I..." The threat of more tears drowned her words. She sniffed and wiped her eyes. "I'm sorry. I'm not usually like this."

"We all deal with stress in different ways. What's your father's status?"

"It's still touch and go."

"What happened? Heart attack? Seizure? Stroke? A fall?"

The woman sighed. "An overdose."

Ava didn't know what to say. "Sometimes seniors feel so lonely that...they don't want to be here anymore."

The woman laughed bitterly. "No, it wasn't a suicide attempt. I probably could handle that better than this. No, my father's an addict. He's been addicted to opiates after he'd gotten a prescription due to a back injury. He's been fighting this addiction for years now. Some years are better than others. It's been months and I thought he was getting better. Then I get a call..."

"I am sorry."

"Aside from my sister, I'm the only one he has left. He's lost friends; some due to death, others couldn't handle how the addiction has changed him. My mother lives with her sister now. The addiction destroyed a once happy marriage of nearly fifty years." She then talked about the man her father used to be and shared childhood memories of him. She mourned the tight-knit family she'd lost and discussed the stress it had put on her own marriage and children. She sighed. "Sorry to burden you. You must be here for your own reasons."

"It's okay," Ava said undisturbed. She was used to listening. "I'm visiting a friend who's quickly recovering." Not a complete lie.

"Glad to hear that." She glanced at Ava's hand. "I see you're engaged."

Ava awkwardly twisted the ring on her finger. Not sure how much longer it would remain there. She now knew why Folu hadn't been acting like himself the past several weeks. She'd busied herself with Gwen's wedding preparations and pretended not to notice. "Yeah, he's great."

"He's lucky to have someone as caring as you."

I wish he thought so instead of finding me scary. "I'm lucky to have him."

The woman opened her mouth then stopped when she noticed a black man in blue scrubs scanning the courtyard. He spotted her and walked over to her with a smile.

"Oh, there you are," the nurse said. "We'd thought you'd gone. You can see your father now."

"Thank you. I'll be right there."

The nurse nodded and left.

Ava stood. "Well I'm glad—," she began then gasped when the woman embraced her in a hug so fierce she was certain she'd heard a rib crack.

"Thank you so much," the woman said.

Ava awkwardly hugged her back, surprised she still managed to breathe. "But I haven't done anything."

"You don't know how much you did for me." She took a step back, wiping her tears. "It's not many people who would listen to a stranger like you did. At one of the lowest points in my life I didn't feel alone." She searched her handbag then pulled out a card. She handed it to her. "If you ever need a favor, don't hesitate to call."

"Alexis Taylor" resembled nothing of the wealthy sounding name or the raised silver letters on her fine linen business card. "I will," Ava said, having no intention of ever doing so.

Alexis waved then hurried inside.

Ava sat back down and munched on her snack wondering whether to return to the reception or go back to the Adesinas. Neither prospect excited her.

Her cell phone rang. She looked at the unfamiliar number then answered.

"Your son's here," a deep voice said on the other line then gave her the address.

"M-my son? I'm afraid you have the wrong number."

"He told me you would say that, but he insists this is the right one."

"He did?"

"Yes. And if I were you I'd get here as soon as you can."

5
____

THERE WAS ONLY a slight chance anyone would think Donovan Lartey looked even remotely like Ava's son.

It certainly wouldn't be from the spiky black hair. Perhaps the brown eyes and plump lips but the toasted coconut skin and hooded gaze were entirely his father's. But unless a Nigerian ancestor, many generations ago, had made their way to Asia somehow, which wasn't impossible but highly unlikely, and intermingled with someone there, also not impossible but highly unlikely, they were light years apart in the looks department.

Donovan ran over to her and leaped at her as if he expected her to catch him, which she did with an "Oof." He was big for seven but hadn't realized it yet, although he was already taller than most of his classmates. He was a child full of energy. He beamed up at her. "Mom!"

Ava didn't smile back, too stunned that this was happening. One moment she was at a hospital now she was in the cramped, metallic paint-scented office of a junkyard manager because a sneaky kid had made his way through a gap in the chain link fence and jumped in the front seat of an old Cadillac.

Her arms instinctively hugged him back before she set him on the ground. Her eyes saying *What have you done now?*

His cherubic smile stayed in place.

"It's really dangerous to have a child wandering around like that," the manager said. A grim faced man, who looked to be in his sixties, with skin so smooth he appeared as if he were wearing foundation.

"I'm sorry."

"This is not a playground. He could have been hurt any number of ways. You're lucky we didn't call Child Protective Services."

Ava felt her face burn at the scolding. She wasn't used to getting in trouble. It was something she actively avoided. But this devilish little imp had put her in the middle of it.

The man continued to chide her and she felt her face getting hotter and hotter and soon her temper began to flare. Before she let it get the best of her she knew the rational thing to do was to disarm him.

She slowly got down on one knee. Donovan gasped in alarm, knowing what she was about to do. "No, please don't," he said, his voice rising in panic.

She ignored him and lowered her other knee and bowed her head, in the most subservient way she could imagine, before she calmly said, "Yes. It won't happen again."

She didn't see the man's face but saw his boots shift back quickly in alarm. "No, no it's okay. It's nothing." He released a nervous laugh. "At least everything is okay. I'll leave you to it then. Give you a minute alone." He pointed at Donovan. "Listen to your mother. If mine was alive she'd have my hide for a stunt like this." He hurried out of the office.

Donovan sighed annoyed. "You didn't have to do that. Especially not to him," he said with childish disgust.

Ava lifted her gaze and looked at him. They were at eye level now. He flinched and wrung his hands. "Please don't be angry. I didn't know who else to call."

"You have a father."

He shifted his feet and scratched his cheek.

"And a grandmother." She knew calling his mother wasn't an option.

Donovan chewed his lower lip then flung his arms around her neck. "And you. I'm so glad you came. You look nice and smell like popcorn. Do you have any left?"

"No." She pulled him away. "And flattery's not going to fix things."

"Were you at a party?"

"Doesn't matter."

"Can't you keep this between us?"

"Donovan."

He clasped his hands together. "Please, Sandy." That nickname always seemed to soften her heart. He'd just started to talk and both she and his father agreed that he couldn't call her by her given name due to their cultures, but she didn't want to be called 'Auntie Ava' (it reminded her too much of a long gone family elder, Aunty Ada, who always managed to smell like burnt chicken and went on about her painful bunions) so instead, his father, Dai, came up with the name Aunty Sandy based on the squirrel Sandy Cheeks from the cartoon *SpongeBob SquarePants*. He told her the cartoon was Donovan's favorite but Ava secretly knew the show had been Dai's and something he wanted to share with his son. In the past two years she'd allowed Donovan to reduce it to just Sandy.

"Depends." Ava rose to her feet.

He frowned. "What does that mean?"

"It means I'll see." She dusted off her dress. "How did you even get here?"

"Bus," he said simply as if that one word answer explained everything. He took her hand and tugged her towards the door. "So where's your car? Can I sit in the front seat?"

"No."

"Can we get some ice cream or candy? I've got some money. I can pay."

"I'd better get you home."

"I'm not supposed to go home yet. Dad's still working."

How like Dai to be working on a weekend. But as the owner of a successful business, she knew he didn't work regular hours. However, sometimes she worried about him working too much. "Where are you supposed to be?"

He threw his head back and groaned. "At a stupid birthday party."

"Then how did you end up here? And the parents didn't—"

"I told them my dad had to pick me up early and I went outside and no one noticed."

"And you decided to get on a bus."

He shrugged. "I've done it before but I've never ridden one to the end of the line."

"You should have stayed at the bus depot and gotten another bus back."

"I know but then I heard this loud noise and I looked across the street and saw this huuuuge crane lift up a refrigerator and I wanted to get a closer look. There's so much stuff here. Piles of stuff. You know Dad once took me to the recycle center but that wasn't even close! Oh, wait, look what I found." He dug into his backpack and pulled out a handle. "What do you think it is?"

"It's for a window." She remembered her grandfather's old station wagon.

He frowned. "The window?"

"When cars didn't have automatic windows, you had to roll them up with this."

"Wow. Like a hand crank for a phonograph. I saw one of those in a museum."

"Yes," Ava said amused, "but it's not as old as that."

"Oh and I found this too," he said holding out a green glass bottle. "Isn't it pretty? When I clean it I'll add it to my collection."

Donovan had a lot of strange collections. He reminded her a little of her half-sister Maya; an artist, who as a teenager, used to use cut fruit and sponges to create prints on her bedroom wall. But Donovan didn't make prints. He built strange structures that most times only made sense to him.

"It's a nice shape."

He gasped and stared at her with wide eyes. "You see it too? It's got a robot body right? I'm gonna add a head and everything when I get home. I can't wait to show you when I'm finished."

"I look forward to that," she said and meant it. One of the few things she didn't have to lie about today. She liked his creative mind.

"I love you, Sandy. So much."

Ever since he'd said those words at about three years old he hadn't stopped. Ava kept waiting for him to grow out of it. But he didn't seem eager to. He was very open with his feelings and she doubted she was the only person he said it to. He was exuberant about most things. He loved cherry pie with loads of whipped cream with the same fervor. She accepted his enthusiastic statement as part of him.

She ruffled his hair. "I love you too."

Soon he was safely seated in the back of her yellow Kia, a car her mother called "cute but undignified," urging her to trade it in for something more suitable for her profession, as a child psychotherapist. No one knew she'd cut back on her client load and was struggling with a tiny crisis of faith about whether she was in the right field or not.

She glanced at her clock. It was almost seven but still bright out. She could get him back home in about forty minutes. His father should be off work by then, but she wouldn't tell him that.

She started the ignition. "So what's your plan now?"

"Plan?"

"You're supposed to be at a birthday party. Isn't that where your father is supposed to pick you up?"

"Oh yeah. Um actually...I sorta lied."

She studied him in the rearview mirror. "Lied?"

He nodded.

"More than telling a stranger that I'm your mother?"

He nodded again.

Ava shut off the ignition, and took a deep breath before she turned to him and said, "Okay. What's really going on?"

Donovan gripped his hand into a fist and said in a quiet voice, "I ran away from Dad's girlfriend."

6

———————

That obnoxious little brat was going to ruin everything! How could she have met the perfect man and have such a foe? Dai was handsome, funny, smart, successful. He had just one teeny tiny little flaw—he adored his son.

A troublemaking little monster.

Elena swore as she drummed her manicured nails against the steering wheel. She'd only left him alone for a couple hours and this was how he repaid her?

He'd nearly made a fool out of her. She'd had to pretend to know that his father had picked him up from the party. Laughing with the parents about being so busy she'd forgotten that fact, before jumping back in her silver Mercedes, driving three blocks away and releasing a primal scream.

Donovan had disappeared on purpose when she'd gone out of her way to be nice to him. This was the thanks she got?! So he was seven and it was a party for five year olds. So what? He'd get pizza and cake, what kid wouldn't want that? Seven years old wasn't that far from five, right?

Dai had been so excited when she'd offered to take

Donovan with her, giving them a chance to bond. Okay, so she left him alone at the party after about five minutes. Although little Anna was adorable, her mother was truly a bore, whose only attribute was that she'd married well and had great contacts Elena planned to exploit in the future. She'd told the kid to mingle and make friends then left him.

Elena parked her car and searched her mind on what to do next. She should have put a tracker on the kid. How could he do this to her? She was usually good with kids. She glanced at her face in the rearview mirror and ran anxious fingers over her maple brown skin. Oh God, he'd give her worry creases. She was too beautiful for this kind of stress. She deserved better.

He probably wasn't far. She might find him walking one of the side streets of the pleasant neighborhood that touted itself as being a unique suburban subdivision. But all the houses looked the same, which turned her around more often than not.

One house she'd passed three times, its main distinction being a string of holiday lights kept on from last year. Then she remembered her friend telling her about a small park built within the division with a walking trail and swings. One of those landscaped places that looked impressive, but was small enough to walk across in minutes. This upper middle class neighborhood was not as impressive as the gorgeous area where Dai lived. Every time she spotted the blue stone walkway and meticulously designed landscaping as she drove up the long driveway to his six bedroom house, she knew she was where she belonged. With Dai.

But first she had to find his son. He had to be at the park.

But he wasn't.

After fifteen minutes of searching and no sign of him Elena pounded the steering wheel. Would she really have to call the police? How would that make her look? What would Dai think of her? No, she had to look a little longer, it was still light out.

Her cell phone rang.

Her heart fell. What if it was Dai? What could she tell him? Where the hell was that stupid little— She looked at the number and her pulse increased for another reason.

She didn't remember giving Ava her number. What could *she* want? Should she ignore it? Elena lifted her finger to deny the call then stopped.

What if because Ava couldn't reach her she called Dai instead? No, that was the last thing she'd want. Elena brightened her voice determined not to sound as if she was having a meltdown. "Hello?"

"I've got Donovan."

That little sh— "Oh thank goodness. I was so worried. Is he okay?"

"He's fine," Ava said, sounding efficient and matter of fact, helping Elena's heart rate return back to normal.

"I'm so relieved. Okay, I'll come and get him." She didn't want to but knew that was the expected thing to say.

"No, it's too far away. I'll meet you at Dai's house. We should be there in another twenty minutes."

"Twenty minutes? Where are you?"

"Donovan hopped on a bus and fell asleep. The bus took him to the end of the line. We're heading back now."

Somehow Elena sensed there was more to the story, but didn't care to find out. At least the kid was safe and sound and if she played her cards right, Dai never had to know what had happened.

"Okay, I'll meet you there." She disconnected the call then sat back in her seat. She took a deep breath, checked her reflection again to make sure she was perfectly calm.

Remaining calm was vital. Frown lines caused wrinkles.

◊

THE FIRST TIME Elena Cardoza met Ava Kayode she wondered about the best way to get rid of her.

The thought resurfaced as her Mercedes made its way up the long driveway and settled behind Ava's lemon yellow car.

She didn't know how Ava managed to arrive at Dai's house before she did.

Although she knew that Dai had zero romantic interest in the cheery faced woman, as Elena watched Ava step out of her car dressed as if she were coming from a party, she found the other woman a threat. Not because she was particularly beautiful, Elena knew she had the upper hand in that department, or particularly successful, she was only moderately so, even that the little hellion seemed to like her didn't disturb Elena much.

What bothered her most was that Ava still existed in Dai's life while other girlfriends had come and gone, plus an ex-wife who stayed conveniently absent. Friends like Ava could be tricky. So her precious Dai was bracketed by two potential threats to her happiness. She'd manage to get rid of them both eventually. Right now she'd use one over the other.

Thankfully, Ava was engaged and Elena hoped she'd get married soon and start a family and be too busy to be by Dai's side.

Elena smoothed down her recently pressed, waist length black hair, before she rushed over to them, her hand over her heart, hoping she looked suitably distressed. "Do you know how worried I've been?"

"You must have been," Ava said. She nudged the quiet boy beside her. "What do you say?"

Donovan bowed his head looking contrite. "Sorry, Ms. Cardoza."

Elena struggled not to grit her teeth. "I told you to call me Elena." More than once.

"He doesn't feel comfortable calling adults by their first names," Ava said.

She knew that. She didn't care. "He can feel comfortable with me." She shifted her attention to Ava. "You really got me out of a tight bind. I don't know how to thank you."

"There's no need for that."

She took out her cell phone. "Do I need to compensate you for gas or—?"

"Um...Elena," Donovan said.

"Quiet, it's rude to interrupt adults when they're talking."

"I know but—"

"What is it?" Ava said.

Elena hated how Ava indulged him. The kid just wanted attention. "Haven't you caused enough trouble?"

He started to bounce up and down looking anxious. "I know, but—"

"Oh, do you need to go to the bathroom?"

He shook his head then pointed to something behind her.

"What is it?" Elena snapped at the end of her patience.

That's when she heard the sound of the smooth engine, the soft glide of tires coming up the driveway and dread swept through her. She knew what he was going to say and didn't want to hear it.

"Dad's home."

7

———

THERE WERE few men who could step out of an innocent looking black BMW hybrid and look like the sexy villain in a graphic novel.

Dai Lartey managed to do so in clothes that would make another man look unremarkable. Faded jeans cascaded over well-formed legs, a plain green T-shirt stretched across his chest, emphasizing the swell of his light cocoa colored biceps. With his wide shoulders, cleanly shaven head and snake tattoo on his neck and his son's name on his left forearm arm, he little resembled a hard driven entrepreneur who owned a business that designed a device he wasn't at liberty to tell anyone about. He just liked to tell people that he dealt with transportation and safety.

If Ava hadn't known him since high school she might have been intimidated by the chiseled jaw he'd gotten from his Ghanaian father and full lips and eyes he'd inherited from his Japanese-American mother as most were when they first saw him. She didn't go for the bulky, muscular types and he could look mean.

But the sight of him usually made her smile. This time the sight of him made her groan.

He approached them with suspicion. "What's going on?"

Donovan rushed forward and hugged him. "Hi, Dad."

The attempt to distract his father didn't work. Dai absently patted his son on the back but didn't break his stride. His gaze focused on one thing—her.

Elena tried to do what Donovan hadn't managed to. She flicked her hair over her shoulder and sauntered over to him like a beautiful lioness. She rested a hand on his chest, before pressing a kiss on his cheek. "You're back early."

Dai's stride faltered only a fraction, but not enough to stop him.

Ava knew it wouldn't. When Dai wanted answers he didn't stop until he got them. He halted a few feet from her, his dark gaze fixed on her face, making her cheeks grow warm.

"What are you doing here?" he said his voice like the rumble of a summer storm.

"Just thought I'd stop by," Ava said.

His gaze dipped to her dress with such slow, careful deliberation she almost felt as if he were scanning every pattern to memory. Finally his gaze returned to her face. "Isn't today your sister's wedding?"

"Yes."

"Then why are you here?"

"There was an incident. It's complicated."

He frowned. "How complicated?"

Elena took his arm. "I'm sure she'll tell you all about it later, but she must be going."

"She's not going anywhere."

Ava glanced towards the house. "Let's not do this out here."

He nodded and motioned her forward.

She nodded in return and gestured to the door. "No, after you. You have the keys after all."

He turned and Ava knew it was the perfect chance to escape, but as if reading her thoughts, Dai's hand shot out and encircled her arm. "You're not doing that," he said in a low voice.

"I was just going to check something in my car."

He sent her a knowing look, seeing through her lie. He effortlessly pulled her along with him as he walked to the front door. "I'm going to find out what's going on."

"It's nothing," Donovan said.

Dai opened the door and stepped inside, taking off his shoes. "If that's the case explain the car oil smudges on your shirt. The one that is also on Sandy's dress."

Ava silently swore. Somehow when she'd hugged him the oil must have transferred. Dai had an annoying habit of noticing small details others missed.

"I gave him a big hug," she said.

"Where did the oil come from?"

"This is my fault," Elena said, looping her arm through his. "I had car trouble and he must have touched something when I wasn't looking. Anyway, I didn't want you worried in case it was going to take long so I called Ava and asked her to pick Donovan up from the party and then when we got here we were chatting because I needed her help to cook one of your favorites."

He looked at Ava for a long moment then nodded. "Okay."

He hadn't even granted Elena a sideward glance. She knew he sensed deception. She needed to leave now. She sidled towards the door.

The main thing was Donovan was safe at home. She'd scolded him for his treatment of Elena and made him promise not to do it again. The rest was up to Dai, Elena and Donovan.

She no longer needed to be part of this domestic drama. She looked at Elena. "And now that you know how to cook that uh thing I should go."

"No, don't do that." Dai took her arm again. "Stay for dinner."

"I really should go."

"Stay. Pleaaase," Donovan said. He held up her slippers. The soft peach colored ones he'd bought for her, the ones he wouldn't let anyone else use.

Ava's gaze shifted from a look of childish hope, to deep suspicion and finally daggers. One thing was clear. Elena wanted her gone and she didn't want to be there. At least they had that in common. "I don't think uh...there's enough food."

"If you've given her the measuring portions, there will be enough," Dai said. "You always make too much."

Ava hesitated. "No, I can't," she said, then her stomach grumbled.

His gaze sharpened. "You haven't eaten any food yet?"

"I didn't get a chance too. I told you there was an incident."

"Which you can tell me about over dinner."

"It's not something I want to talk about."

His eyes widened and he swore as a thought occurred to him. "I'm sorry. I'm an idiot. Did the wedding even happen? Did Gwen get stood up?"

"No, thankfully not. It wasn't that." She glanced at Donovan before she looked at Dai and said in a slow, firm tone. "I said I'll tell you later."

Dai finally got the hint and nodded. "Okay. You're still not leaving until you've eaten something."

"I ate off the rest of her caramel popcorn," Donovan said. "At first she said no but then she said yes and I know why. It tasted a little stale."

"Go wash up and change your shirt."

Donovan turned to Ava. "Are you staying for dinner?"

"It will be a pleasure to have you join us," Elena added, every word a lie.

Ava took off her heels and slid into the slippers suppressing a moan of pleasure. It was a relief to get out of her heels and the slippers hugged her feet like a warm blanket. "I guess I am staying then. I can help you in the kit—"

"No, I'm fine," Elena said. Behind Dai's head she mouthed "Keep him busy" then disappeared into the kitchen.

Donovan began to head to his bedroom, but Dai grabbed the back of his collar and stopped him. "How was the birthday party?"

"Fine."

Dai paused. "Just fine?"

Ava felt her pulse quicken. In Donovan's world few things were fine. They were *amazing* or *horrible*, *spectacular* or a *disaster*. Donovan's lukewarm response was a cause for concern. She couldn't let Dai get any more suspicious than he already was. "He's already told me all the amazing things that went on that he's run out of things to say," she said.

Dai kept his gaze fixed on Donovan. "That's rare."

"It was a baby party," Donovan said.

"Yes, but you were a trooper, right? Didn't cause any mayhem?"

Ava laughed, "Except for face planting into the cake, no."

Dai sent her a look. "That's not funny."

"The birthday girl didn't think so either. There were tears."

He narrowed his eyes. "Still not funny."

"Nothing happened." She sent Donovan a pointed look. "And nothing will happen again, right?"

He nodded. "Right."

Ava smiled at Dai putting on her most innocent expression. "So nothing to worry about."

He fell for it, as most people did, and released Donovan's collar. "Hmm."

"Now go change your shirt like your father told you to. And wash your hands."

Dai opened his mouth and Ava knew he had a series of questions she wasn't ready to answer yet so she said, "The kitchen sound awfully quiet. Let me go check on Elena and see if she needs any help."

She left before Dai could stop her.

Only problem, Elena wasn't there.

8

———————

EXCEPT FOR A LARGE bowl left on the island in the expansive gourmet kitchen, it didn't look like Elena planned to cook anything at all.

Where was she?

Dai came into the kitchen and waved his cell phone. "She went out to get more ingredients. She'll be back soon."

Ava opened the fridge and saw the rows of food. "What more could she need?"

"She likes to impress. That's just her way."

And why did she sneak out of the kitchen without letting us know? But she wouldn't ask that question. Dai was as suspicious as it was and if he didn't find anything wrong or strange about Elena's behavior she wouldn't point it out to him. She opened a drawer where she knew he kept a chattering teeth toy she liked to wind up and run along the counter when she was stressed. She paused when she saw a red ring box among the extra batteries, markers, and old takeaway menus.

She quickly closed the drawer.

"Did you see it?"

"No."

Dai laughed. "It's okay if you did."

"Why do you have a ring box in our junk drawer?"

"It's supposed to be a surprise. I thought Elena would have found it a week ago."

Dai opened the drawer and held the box out to her.

Ava waved her hands and took a step back. "Elena's supposed to see it, not me."

"I want you to." He opened the box.

She snapped it closed. "It's beautiful."

"You barely looked at it."

"Yellow gold with princess diamonds with the words 'I adore you' engraved inside."

"You did not see all that."

Ava grinned and sent him a superior look. "No, but I know you."

"I'm that predictable."

"No, you're that romantic. She's going to love it."

Dai leaned against the counter and folded his arms. "Do you like her?"

"Does it matter?"

"Of course it matters if I plan to marry her."

"You were planning to marry her anyway."

"Still."

"I hardly know her."

"It's been eight months. You've met her enough times."

I know she can't stand the sight of me. "She seems nice."

"That's not an answer."

"I don't think she'll kill you in your sleep."

He nodded. "That is a requirement."

"Or try to organize your garage."

He nodded again. "Right." He nudged her with his arm

and lowered his head. "Want to know the truth? I forgot I'd put it there."

Ava laughed.

"For the past week I've been trying to remember where I'd hid it and a part of me was terrified she'd find it before I did."

"Because you're not sure?"

"No, because I want to see her face when I give it to her."

Ava hadn't seen her friend look so happy in such a long time. She felt a little jealous. His love life was kicking up while hers was circling the drain.

"Good. So you've found The One?"

"Yes." He wasn't one to smile a lot and he didn't now, but his face glowed with joy and satisfaction. "You've met her. We get on really well and Donovan likes her too. You know that's rare. Somehow he's calm around her."

Donovan wasn't an easy kid to manage. When Donovan had broken his arm after trying to find out if a skirt would act like a parachute, Dai had told her, "Other parents worry about drink and drugs. I just want my kid not to accidentally kill himself."

He looked relaxed and at peace as he thought about Elena and the future ahead of them. She didn't want that to change.

"Well, now you can hire a pilot and have the words written in the sky."

A wistful smile came and went. "I actually thought of it but then decided I wanted to do things differently this time around."

He'd taken his ex-wife up in a hot air balloon then arranged the words 'Will You Marry Me?' in pink, white and red balloons on the ground for her to see. Ava had helped him plan the surprise so she could understand him wanting to be a little more subdued the second time around.

Dai turned and opened the pantry door and began to place the ring high on a shelf.

"What about you and Folu?"

"It's over."

He turned sharply to her. The ring box fell from his hand. "What?"

She hadn't meant to say it. Didn't know why she had. She shook her head in regret. "It's nothing."

"You can't tell me 'It's over' and then say 'It's nothing.' What happened?"

She picked up the ring box, checked to make sure the ring was safely settled inside, then handed it back to him. "Think we should order take out?"

"Ava!"

"He got cold feet." As much as it hurt, it felt good to say it aloud. She could trust Dai not to tell anyone. "He wants to break off the engagement and I want to figure out a way to change his mind."

"How long have you been keeping this from me?"

"I haven't kept anything from you."

"Then when did he tell you this?"

"Today."

His brows shot up. "Today?"

She nodded. "Don't look at me like that. I know it's pathetic to get dumped at your own sister's wedding."

Dai moved to comfort her, but she shook her head and left the pantry. He wanted to hug her, that's what he did, but she didn't want to get too close when she was hiding so much from him. Like the reason Donovan really had oil on his shirt, that his son didn't really like Elena, or even how angry Folu had made her. And if Dai hugged her it would be like being embraced by a truth ring and she may not be able to resist telling him everything that weighted down her heart until she thought it would break.

She knew his arms would be gentle and firm, that he'd smell like the cinnamon buns he liked to munch on.

She pressed her palms on the countertop. The cool marble feeling good as hot tears stung behind her eyes. In the corner of her eye, she saw Dai's rice cooker, a large turquoise machine he'd gotten in the divorce, which reminded her of when his mother used to always have rice on the ready to pour curry on top. She'd never admit that that had been one of her favorite comforting dishes. "I don't know what I did wrong. I don't know why I would make him question—"

She could feel Dai walk up beside her, he placed a tender hand on her shoulder, but she couldn't look at him. "You didn't do anything wrong," he said.

Everything turned blurry. She wiped a tear from her cheek. She was sad but also angry. She gripped her hands into fists. "I'm so close. So close to having everything. My parents will be so disappointed in me."

His hand covered hers, a shocking warmth compared to the cool feel of the countertop. "It's not your fault. What did he say?"

Before she could reply Donovan burst into the room. "I changed my shirt and washed my hands. And did you know Ms. Cardoza's car's gone...Why is Sandy crying?"

"Could you give us a minute, Dynamo?" Dai said.

He wrung his hands distraught. "Did Ms. Cardoza get angry at you?"

Dai's tone sharpened. "Why would she get angry?"

"It's not that." She smiled at the anxious child, hoping to reassure him, silently begging him to say no more. "Everything is okay."

Donovan blinked rapidly before he spun around and ran out the room.

Ava sniffed and wiped her eyes. "I really should go before Elena gets back."

Dai nodded slowly. "Uh huh keep trying to fool yourself that leaving is even a possibility. Make no mistake, I will find out what really happened today, but first tell me about Folu. What did he say?"

They heard something crash in the other room before Donovan shouted, "I'm okay."

Dai softly swore. "I'll be right back." He pointed at her. "Don't leave. Because if you do, I'll find you. Remember, I know where you live."

He left and Ava considered slipping out the way Elena had but she didn't want to. She felt comfortable here. She wasn't ready to return home and pretend everything was okay. And she was hungry. She could buy something and eat it before she got home but didn't feel in the mood. Dai and Donovan proved a good distraction.

Kid's drawings, held up by animal shaped magnets, adored the front of the charcoal colored, French door refrigerator. One picture magnet showed Dai, Donovan and her in front of a Ferris Wheel. Dai sported a black eye, due to a friendly tennis match gone wrong with his cousin Koji; Donovan had lost his two front teeth and Ava had taken the picture but her thumb had partially gotten in the way. She didn't know why Dai hadn't let her edit it out or why he'd kept it. But it had been a fun memory. Once Dai remarried that picture would likely end up in the junk drawer. The thought came with a sense of loss.

Dai returned to the kitchen. "Nothing broken."

"That's a relief."

"Just a structure he'd been trying to make out of binder clips." He waved his hand. "Don't ask." Dai folded his arms, looking like a man ready to start a barroom brawl. "So what did this asswipe tell you?"

"Folu's hardly that."

"Even his name is a four-letter word."

"It's a nickname. Short for--."

"Don't care. Never will." He paused. "But prove me wrong. What did he say?"

"That I make him feel weak. That he doesn't want to get married to me because I make him feel bad about himself."

"You're right. I misjudged him. He's a mother—"

"Stop that."

"What else did he say?"

She hesitated. "He told me he loves me but that I deserve better."

"Hmm."

"You'll have to help me come up with ideas."

"To do what?"

"Win him back."

Dai shook his head. "Nope. I'll help you delete accounts, erase every image you have of him, but not that."

"Why not?"

"Do you really want him back?"

He rested his hands on his hips, sent her a dark challenge.

For a moment she faltered. Briefly, she considered his question. *Do you really want...?* It didn't matter what she wanted. There was so much at stake. "Have you been listening to anything I've just said?" she shot back upset he'd gotten her to waver even a little.

"Only the part about a jerk telling you that you're too strong to marry."

"He didn't say that."

"I'm reading between the lines."

"It was the shock of the accident."

"What accident?"

"Oh, right. I didn't tell you about the wedding."

Another crashing sound filled the room. "I'm alright," Donovan said.

Dai briefly closed his eyes. "Do you mind if we continue this conversation where I can keep a closer eye on him?"

"No," she said relieved. Facing him had become difficult. She needed the reprieve. "Let's go."

THERE WAS little chance of having a quiet, adult conversation with a kid like Donovan around. Ava wasn't going to discuss her broken engagement or trying to change Folu's mind so she decided to talk about the wedding incident.

However, the moment Donovan overheard her talking about someone getting hit by a car he flooded her with questions. Which then led to them sitting on the area rug in the middle of the hardwood flooring of the informal living room, and helping him with the structure he was trying to build, which then led to more questions and before they knew it a half hour had passed.

"I think you should check on her," Ava said.

Dai attached another binder clip to the structure. "Check on who?"

"Shouldn't Elena be back by now? The grocery store isn't that far."

"I'm sure she's fine."

"If she doesn't come soon I'll have to order something. I don't want to go home too late."

"I want egg rolls!" Donovan said.

"You'll eat what Elena fixes us," Dai countered.

Donovan made a face but didn't argue.

Fortunately, Elena returned with bags and hustled into the kitchen begging off any offers of help.

Soon the delicious aroma of ginger and black pepper scented the sound of something sizzling on the stove.

"I'll get dishes and utensils. You keep your eyes on..." Ava motioned to Donovan now absorbed in a puzzle.

"Thanks."

She walked into the kitchen greeted by the sights and smells of a feast: bowls of yellow rice, greens, chopped chicken, rolls. She wondered how Elena had managed to cook so much in such a short period of time. She suspected the other woman might have gotten help from a pre-made meal or two (perhaps even a takeaway), but she wouldn't acknowledge the possible deception.

No matter how she'd accomplished the dinner, Elena had really outdone herself and Ava opened her mouth to tell her so. But then stopped. She noticed Donovan's prescription bottle on the counter. Dai didn't usually keep it in the kitchen.

And there was something unnerving about the way Elena stood hunched over the countertop.

Ava saw Donovan's favorite plate piled high with food. Elena sprinkled white powder all over it.

She then carefully mixed it in.

9

―――――――

AVA HAD SUSPECTED Elena of many things. Perhaps shaving a year or five off her real age, adding to her already generous cleavage, slightly exaggerating her academic background, but she'd never suspected her of drugging a child.

She quickly left the kitchen undetected, her mind racing to figure out what to do next.

She wanted to say something but she knew it was Dai's job to confront Elena not her. What if they'd agreed to it? She didn't want to accuse Dai's girlfriend—the woman he planned to ask to marry him—of anything.

So confronting her was out of the question. She would not jeopardize Elena's relationship with him until she understood more. For now she had to make sure that Donovan didn't eat any of the food on that plate. She had to outwit her somehow.

Ava went back into the living room and saw Donovan's puzzle—the image of a sleek, blue train gliding along a track, taking shape. "That's amazing. You've come so far. You should show Elena."

"But she's busy in the kitchen—" Dai said.

"She needs the break. Let her see what Donovan has done."

Donovan didn't appear overly eager to show Elena but Ava was finally able to convince him to share his progress. Elena made some protest but then they managed to get her out of the kitchen.

Once alone, Ava worked quickly. She threw away the food on Donovan's plate, washed it and then cleaned the utensils. If this was a new habit that Dai knew about (and hadn't told her, which was rare since he basically told her everything) she'd take the blame. But until she was certain, she wasn't going to let Elena do anything against Donovan.

Ava added new food to his plate and carefully arranged it so that it looked as if it hadn't been touched.

Elena came in just as Ava was finishing. "Great job, Elena. Looks like everything is ready. Let's head to the table."

ALL THROUGH DINNER Elena looked like a woman lost at sea. As Donovan chatted, nearly nonstop, Ava looked at Dai and he didn't seem to think anything was amiss.

However...

Elena's annoyance and confusion grew. Ava could imagine her wondering when the drug would take effect, silently willing it to, and Ava had a tiny thrill knowing it never would. But she knew she would have to tell Dai before Elena had a chance to do it again. Perhaps using a stronger dose.

He was in love. She could tell by the way he kept stealing glances at his girlfriend and then smiling at Ava as if to say *"See? Isn't this great?"* and Ava had smiled back as if to say *"Yeah, it is,"* trying not to feel sick.

How could she tell him?

Maybe it was nothing. Maybe it was a harmless supplement.

But, unlike Donovan's recent exploits, leaving a party and ending up at a junkyard, Ava wouldn't keep this to herself. She had to say something. She could understand the temptation. Donovan could be a handful and Elena had said she'd once worked in a pharmacy. But...

"You look worried," Dai said.

Ava glanced at her watch, wanting to cover the cause of her concern. "I really should get going."

"You can spend the night," Donovan said. "You can sleep in my room like Elena sometimes does with Dad."

Elena choked on her drink. Dai shook his head. Ava felt her heart sink. Dai only had sleepovers when he was ready to commit. He was particular who he exposed his son to. He was completely in love with Elena. This was the woman he wanted to spend his life with.

"Maybe another time."

"A sleepover would be fun."

"Why don't I help you get ready for bed?"

He made a face. "It's not the same."

"Or I can leave now."

"Okay, okay."

Elena looked relieved that Ava was giving her and Dai a chance to be alone, but Dai looked at Ava curious.

She smiled to let him know it was okay, but he narrowed his eyes. She wiggled her brows to say *"Relax,"* his mouth softened to a grin.

Ava managed to get Donovan showered and changed without much fanfare, water tended to calm him, then followed him into his spacious bedroom with its soft avocado green walls, colorful artwork and lightly hued bed sheets. Along one wall a large wire bookshelf stood crammed full of toys and games.

Evidence of Dai trying to overcompensate for his ex-wife's absence.

"Are you okay?" Donovan asked her as she pulled the bed sheets up to his chin.

"I have a lot on my mind. But I'm happy to be here with you."

He sat up, the bed sheets fell to his waist. "Elena's mad."

"She has a reason to be."

"Think she'll tell Dad?"

"Maybe."

He looked down, rolled part of the bed sheet in the shape of a sausage. "When I'm with you I feel like myself, but with her I'm tired."

Ava chewed her lip. "Really? How long have you felt like that?"

He shrugged, looked up at her. "I don't know. It's just sometimes it's hard to think."

"Well, I'm glad you're fine now." She gently pushed him down and adjusted the bed sheets over him. "So you'd better sleep."

"Sure you can't spend the night?"

"I'm sure."

He sprung up again. "Can we have egg rolls next time?"

"Yes."

He hugged her. "I love you, Sandy."

"I love you too."

"You...you won't stop being friends with Dad because of me right?"

"Why would you say that?"

He shrugged.

She nudged him. "Come on."

"Dad and Mom fought about me all the time. Sometimes Elena does too. And one time..."

"What?"

He lowered his voice. "Dad doesn't know but I heard one of his girlfriends say he'd be better off without me."

Dai hadn't dated much since his divorce four years ago. There had been two other women before Elena. An interior designer who thought trying to win Ava over would be the quickest way to Dai's heart, popping up at Ava's house unannounced and planning girl dates. Then there'd been the brand manager who could talk more than Donovan could.

She never would have suspected either woman would have said that, but she knew Donovan wasn't one to lie about hurtful comments like that.

"And that's why she's no longer around." She pushed him down and covered him. "You are not to worry about crazy adults. Just be yourself," she tweaked his nose making him giggle, "without getting into too much trouble."

Ava left Donovan's room, careful to leave the door ajar, and leaned against the wall. She and Dai had never argued about Donovan before. But Dai hadn't been in love like this in a long time. She hoped this wouldn't be the first.

10

———

She heard them laughing.

Ava sat at the top of the stairs. If Elena planned to spend the night it would make things awkward. She could leave and talk to him tomorrow but this was urgent. What if she spiked Donovan's breakfast too?

She covered her face and groaned. Today had been a horrible day and the night was going to be ten times worse.

She let her hands fall to her lap when she heard footsteps.

"I'm really sorry about today," she said.

"Why do you apologize for things that aren't your fault?" Dai sat down beside her. "It's safe to cry now."

If only that were true. "Where's Elena?"

He rested his arm around her shoulder and kissed her on the forehead. "I sent her home so you can spend the night if you want to. I know that you don't want to go home yet. You can face your family tomorrow."

He was so considerate. She blinked back tears. She had to be strong. "You might change your mind."

He frowned. "Why would I do that?"

She pushed him away. "Because you may hate me in a minute."

His eyes searched her face. "Why?"

"I...don't know how to tell you this." She closed her eyes. "I'm not even sure I should."

"What?"

He could blame her. He could tell her it was none of her business. He could say she was jealous because he was happy and she wasn't. Except she knew Dai wasn't like that. But he could change to protect someone special to him...

"Ava? What's going on?"

She pressed a finger to her lips then motioned to the bottom of the stairs.

She took his hand and led him into the living room. "You should probably sit down."

The wine colored sofa was usually their favorite spot. She remembered helping him chose it after his ex-wife left him taking the designer furniture with her. Ava and Dai ended up choosing a hardy, yet comfortable, stain resistant couch that suited a child like Donovan and made the housekeeper's job easy.

Dai sat down, his gaze never leaving her face. "You're starting to scare me."

He turned to her when she sat down next to him. "I know and I'm sorry," she said, "but... have you and Elena decided to change how Donovan takes his medicine?"

"Change how?"

"I don't know. A new routine, perhaps."

"No. What is this about?"

"This evening..." She paused. Took a deep breath. "I saw Elena putting something in Donovan's food." She paused when she sensed him become still. That wasn't a good sign.

"Go on," Dai said in a deceptively soft voice.

"I know he takes his medicine at certain times and I wouldn't have thought much of it if I hadn't seen his prescription on the table and his was the only plate she was, um, adding it to."

Dai didn't move. He barely blinked. He barely breathed. He stared at her.

Ava waited for him to deny it. To tell her that she didn't know what she'd seen. That she had to be mistaken. Instead his eyes turned dark then slowly filled with tears.

She remembered that same expression when he'd learned a beloved uncle had been hit by a drunk driver on one of his early morning bike rides. She remembered holding Dai's hand when he learned the handsome man with a big laugh, who loved dirty jokes and watching baking competitions had died from his injuries.

She felt as if someone he'd loved had died again, and, in a way, they had. The woman he'd loved was not who he'd thought she was.

Ava watched the pool of tears spill down his face. He didn't move to wipe them away. He didn't move at all. He just stared at her without really seeing her anymore. His mind was far away.

She looked around for a tissue box and began to stand.

He grabbed her wrist. "Please, don't go."

"I wasn't going to. I was just..." She let her words fade because he wasn't listening. His gaze shifted to Donovan's puzzle. His legs bounced up and down and he clenched and unclenched his other hand.

He rubbed his forehead then clenched his hand again. "The woman I want to marry has been drugging my son?"

"I think so."

"How long do you think she's been doing it?"

"Well, I know she didn't do it tonight. She tried. But I

didn't let her. I distracted her and then cleaned the plate so Donovan didn't take any of it."

He nodded slowly then repeated. "How long do you think she's been doing it?"

"I don't know," Ava said feeling helpless.

"But you can guess."

"Tonight Donovan told me he's usually tired when she's around and that he sometimes has trouble thinking."

"So it could have been months."

"Yes."

He gulped ominously then politely said, "Excuse me," before he walked into the bathroom and lost his dinner. She heard the toilet flush, water rushing into the sink, then his footsteps heading upstairs. Moments later she heard him in the kitchen. The sound of ice clinking into a glass followed, then she heard more rushing water.

She closed her eyes and imagined him taking a long swallow of ice cold water, hoping it would help him.

He returned to the living room and paced. He'd changed his T-shirt (he now wore one that was dark blue and sleeveless) and he smelled minty like mouthwash. But pacing didn't calm him. Instead, he grew more and more agitated.

"Dai, sit down."

"I didn't protect my son."

"Dai—"

"What kind of father am I?"

"A great one."

He sniffed. "Really? I didn't notice a thing."

"You wouldn't have."

He glared at her. "I wouldn't have noticed a woman drugging my son into submission?" He slapped his forehead. "I am such an idiot. I thought she had a calming effect on him. It was one of the reasons why..." He swore.

"Dai, it's okay."

He sent her a sharp look, his voice rising. "It's not okay. This happened in my house!"

"Shh! You'll wake Donovan."

Dai stripped off his shirt, gathered it into a ball and screamed into it.

"Dai."

He screamed again.

"I'm really sorry," Ava said, not knowing what else to say.

He stood shirtless in front of her, the snake tattoo on his neck looking ready to bite. "So will you tell me the truth?"

"I just did."

"About what really happened today?"

She wouldn't tell him. He didn't need to know the truth. He'd suffered enough. He was worried enough about Donovan, he didn't need to know anymore than was necessary. Ava sighed, pretended she'd been caught in a lie and said, "Donovan left the birthday party and hopped on a bus until it reached the end of the line and then got off and roamed around the bus depot picking up 'treasures.' The manager called me when she spotted him."

Dai hung his head and squeezed his eyes shut. "Lord give me strength."

"At least he didn't get hurt."

He stared up at the ceiling, exasperated. "You'd find the bright side to a plague."

"It's true. It could have been worse."

He kept his gaze fixed on the ceiling. "Hmm."

"Elena was rightfully in a panic. We planned to meet her and act as if nothing had happened but then..."

He met her eyes. "I came home early."

"Exactly."

"Glad I did. Otherwise I may never have known that she

was…" He shook his head. "I can't believe I didn't see it." He paused. "But now that I think about it sometimes Donovan just seemed 'off.'"

"You would have never suspected a thing. I wouldn't have if I hadn't seen it with my own eyes so don't blame yourself."

He put his T-shirt back on and sat down beside her. "I can't help it."

He looked so devastated that tears stung her eyes. She'd never wanted to hurt him this much.

He surprised her by taking her hand and kissing the back of it. He'd done it before but this time felt different, filled with more emotion and tenderness than it ever had before. "Thank you," he said in a raw whisper.

She swallowed. "But I—"

"Don't dismiss what you did today. It took courage. The kind of courage Folu couldn't take. I'm glad you have it. I'm glad you…" He took a deep, steadying breath, held her gaze. "You're one of the few people I can trust. I can trust you with my life and my son's life and I don't say that lightly."

"I know."

"So when I say 'thank you' just accept it."

Ava lowered her head. "Then why do I feel so miserable? As if I let you down? You were so happy only an hour ago."

"I'm still happy. I'm happy you're here."

She lifted her head. "What are you going to do now?"

"What do you think?"

"But you have no proof. You only have my word."

Chilled anger touched his brown eyes. Ava inwardly shivered glad it wasn't directed at her. "Your word is all I need."

11

———

HE WASN'T HERE for sex.

Elena knew Dai could look mean. A little scary. It was what she found sexy about him. But this evening his eyes were cold enough to freeze off someone's fingers.

She grabbed the collar of her pink satin robe, still aroused enough to want to have him rip it off her if he so desired. Underneath she wore her favorite lacy bra and panty set.

His text had said *I need to see you* and she was willing to give him plenty to see. "Come in."

"I'm not sure," he began. He gripped his hand into a fist, sighed then finally said, "Okay," and stepped inside her apartment.

He was acting strange. But she was so glad to see him that it didn't matter. He'd chosen her over Ava. She'd been so annoyed when he'd refused her offer to stay with him. But now he was here. He was still hers. She knew the taste of his soft lips, his thick thighs pressed against hers. His hard—

"I'll give you three seconds to come clean about Donovan's medicine."

Elena blinked, the lovely image bursting like a soap bubble. "Whose medicine?"

He rested his hands on his hips. "Donovan. Have you been sneaking extra doses into his food?"

She swallowed. He was never supposed to know about that. She'd never wanted him to. She gestured to the camel colored sofa she was still paying off. Seeing him sit there always made each payment worth it. "Why don't you sit down? I'll get you something to drink."

He shook his head. "If I sit down it'll be worse."

"What do you mean?"

"Because I'll know when you're lying. You know me, I'll become hyper focused and focus on your every movement. So it's better we stand."

"I don't know why you would suspect me of such a thing."

"That's not an answer."

"I don't know where this is coming from."

"Ava saw you so stop playing games and tell me the truth."

Ava, that bitch! "She's lying. She didn't see anything. She just wants—"

"Stop right there," he interrupted, sending her a look so vicious fear touched her heart. His voice remained cordial, but tinged with menace. "I'm angry right now. You don't want to push me."

"Why would you believe her over me?" She stepped closer, rested a hand on his chest, gazed up into his eyes. "Don't you love me?"

She felt him weakening. Butterflies of delight swirled within her. She inhaled his scent, he smelled so good, like he'd just stepped out of the shower, his skin held the scent of mint and fresh tangerine. She hoped to get him out of this foul mood and into her bed.

"I would do anything for you."

"What took you so long with shopping?"

She hesitated. That was not what she'd expected him to say. "The store was busy."

Ava again! Damn her. "Ava said she saw you crushing pills."

"That's impossible, baby. I told you she was a liar. It was a small capsule."

"I see."

It was only when he smiled, an expression that made her blood go cold, that she realized her mistake.

"What else did Ava lie about?"

Elena nervously stroked her hair. "She doesn't like me. She doesn't want us to be together. Don't you see?"

Dai closed his eyes. "What was in the capsule?"

"It's not his medicine."

He looked at her. "What is it?"

"It calms him."

He folded his arms.

Elena felt her unease increase. When some men folded their arms they might look tense or upset. Dai looked like a man who could blow up a city, keep his footing during the blast, and then smile as he wiped ash from his face. "What is it?" he asked in a too soft voice. "A supplement? A mineral?"

"A low dose variation of what he takes. I've done tons of research and it's incredibly safe."

"Then why didn't you tell me?"

"I did but—"

"But what?"

"You wouldn't listen," she said, remembering her sense of desperation. Dai was perfect but she hadn't been able to manage Donovan and her plan was such a simple and easy solution. "You dismissed the idea. You didn't want him on any more meds than you thought necessary."

"So you went behind my back."

"It's harmless and it works. It makes everyone happy and—"

"How long?"

"Not long. You don't know what it's like. I've tried to be there for him but he doesn't make it easy and I know it's not his fault. I am helping him. Helping us. You were so stressed before. I was trying to help." She rested a hand on his chest. "Baby, I'm so sorry. I realize what I did was wrong, but I love you so much and I know how much he worries you."

He stepped away from her and Elena felt the loss of their connection as she met his gaze, darkened by the pain of betrayal. "You don't know how much you hurt me."

"I'm sorry." She'd never regretted something so much in her life. She gripped his shirt, desperate not to lose him. "Truly. I never meant to hurt you. I promise I won't do it again."

He removed her hand and turned to the door. "There's no need to promise because you'll never get the chance to."

Somehow having Ava wait up for him made it worse. She'd stayed so that he wouldn't leave Donovan alone when he went to see Elena, but he'd expected to find her asleep. It would have been easier coming back to a dimly lit house. To be left alone to wallow in his anger, humiliation and sadness.

"Donovan's still asleep," she said, greeting him at the door.

"Hmm."

He didn't want to talk. But the moment she began to gather her things, he realized he didn't want to see her leave.

"Please stay. I won't be able to sleep tonight."

"I can drug your ginger tea," she said then cringed. "Sorry, bad joke."

"Really bad."

She groaned. "I know. Forget I said anything."

"I will if you stay."

"Well, there's a surprise for you in the kitchen."

"I don't think I can take any more surprises."

"You'll like this one."

He went into the kitchen, opened the fridge and found a square shaped glass bowl. He lifted the lid and revealed an egg sandwich.

"I thought you might be hungry."

He picked up one half of the sandwich and bit down into the pillowy soft Japanese milk bread and let the creamy, rich egg mixture settle on his tongue. "This is why I love you," he said before he took another large bite.

The simple sandwich had been a favorite from childhood. It didn't include anything fancy like onions, lettuce, or mustard. Just mashed boiled eggs between bread. Simple and delicious.

"Slow down or you might choke," she said.

"You made two, right?" he mumbled around another large bite.

"Of course."

He took another bite and it didn't feel like enough. It tasted better than anything he'd ever had before. Creamer, sweeter, softer than any memory he could muster.

Then he realized why. Because of her. Because Ava had made it for him after suffering heartbreak at her sister's wedding; after having to pick up his son and deal with his now *ex*-girlfriend; after staying here late so that he could confront Elena, changing out of her beautiful outfit into one of his T-shirts and a pair of drawstring sweatpants. In spite of all that, she'd taken the time to think of him and make this sandwich.

He stared down at the empty bowl. He'd walloped most of the sandwich down without care. It didn't matter how hungry he'd been. He hadn't taken the time to sit down and truly savor and enjoy the effort she'd put into it.

He stared at her fresh face and realized how precious and dear she was to him. He knew that, but tonight, somehow he felt it a hundred times more. This time he didn't want to kiss her hand he wanted to kiss *her*. Because she didn't make him feel foolish or stupid. The way she looked at him never wavered; whether he succeeded or failed she always looked at him as if he was okay. That there wasn't something wrong with him. That he was fine as he was—flaws and all.

Few people made him feel that way. And he wanted to kiss her to show her how beautiful she was, how amazing.

"Is something wrong?" she asked.

Yes. "No." He popped the last bite of the sandwich into his mouth.

She turned to the fridge. "On to number two."

"No, not tonight. I'll have it another time."

She faced him concerned. "You didn't like it?"

"I did. That's why I want to make the second one last." He licked mayo off his thumb. "And Folu was right. He doesn't deserve you."

12

―――――

She refused to believe it was over.

Elena sat in her car and watched the Kayode house. Sensible people usually stalked their exes.

But she preferred to stalk the cause: The other woman who had destroyed her chance at happiness.

It was Ava's fault that Dai wouldn't accept her calls or answer her texts. It was Ava's fault that Dai wouldn't give her a chance to explain.

Ava had always been a threat. She'd underestimated her.

She hated being wrong.

To think she'd actually cooked for that woman.

Elena saw Ava coming up the block smiling at someone on her phone. She usually took a quick walk around the block with some plain looking, skinny chick. She'd already learned her habits.

But she felt rage building. All that she'd hoped for and dreamed about, this deceptively kind looking woman had stolen from her.

This woman who already had it all. Aside from a loving

family, she got to stay in their gorgeous house with them, while Elena's parents tried to squeeze four adults and five kids into a three bedroom apartment because they were kind but too simple to know that hard work didn't get you very far and constantly helping extended family could be a burden not a blessing.

Elena'd had to scrimp and save to get a degree. Ava had gotten a partial scholarship (like the bitch needed one!) and help from her wealthy parents.

With Dai, Elena's life had changed. It had been a true fairy tale. There had been multiple trips to the Caribbean, dinners at fine restaurants, dancing, gifts. He was so generous with gifts. The jewelry, the flowers, the clothes—no other man had ever spoiled her the way he had. Dai had meant a ticket to a new life.

She feared she'd never get a chance like this again. Other men found her a little too demanding; Dai had never had a problem with that. He was so easygoing and generous. Anything she asked for he was willing to get for her.

She glanced at the gold bracelet on her wrist. She'd expected a ring next and no doubt Dai would have proposed if someone hadn't gotten in her way.

She gripped the steering wheel her rage continuing to grow. Then Ava laughed.

The horrible woman threw her head back and laughed.

As if she were laughing at her.

Elena remembered being laughed at in high school when another girl exposed that her designer backpack was a knock off. When a guy she'd liked told everyone her father used to be his family's gardener. Had Ava been laughing at her the entire time? Did she think she was better than her?

Elena couldn't stand it any longer. Her growing rage turned

into fury. She couldn't stand the pain of losing him, of how much she missed him. She and Dai were meant to be together.

She lightly fingered the delicate bracelet before she carefully took it off and placed it in the glove compartment. Then she took off her earrings.

She'd once gotten kicked out of a high school for punching a teacher for disrespecting her. She opened the car door and let that angry, rebellious teenager take control.

13

———

The attack was fierce and unexpected.

One moment Ava was walking to her house, while on a video call with Donovan, and the next she was on the ground with a screaming banshee on top of her.

"I could kill you. You ruined everything!" Elena said. "Why did you have to tell him? Why didn't you talk to me first?"

It was only because she was so startled that Elena managed to get so many blows in—Ava managed to block her face, but Elena got in three punches; in the chest, one in the side, one on her arm—but then Ava was able to assess the situation. She swiftly elbowed Elena in the throat, causing her to choke.

Ava rolled away.

"Sandy! Sandy!" she heard Donovan shouting.

"It's okay." She tried to turn the phone off so that Donovan couldn't see or hear what was happening, but Elena got in front of her and absently kicked it way out of reach.

"You owe me," she said.

Ava rushed to her feet. "I don't know what—"

"You have everything." Elena spread her arms wide. "You're engaged to a great guy, you've got a family who loves you and a career and Dai as a friend." She shoved her. "But that wasn't enough. You had to take him away from me."

Ava stumbled back. "You did that on your own."

She shoved her again. Harder. "You didn't have to say anything. You know that."

"Stop it, Elena."

She shoved her again, but this time Ava didn't move. "He never needed to know," Elena said. "I would have stopped. I would never hurt Donovan."

Ava held up her hands. "This is not the way to handle things."

"You can make it right. Talk to him. Make him understand."

"No."

"Otherwise he won't get what he wants."

"You're threatening him?"

Elena raised her hand to slap her, but Ava grabbed her wrist and twisted it. Elena gasped in shock and stared at Ava as if she'd witnessed a cute poodle turn into a shark.

"Leave them alone," Ava warned then released her grip.

Elena rubbed her wrist blinking back tears of anger and pain. "He's going to regret choosing you over me. He doesn't know what he's giving up. He'll find out how much he needs me." She turned and stormed away.

DAI RARELY HAD a chance to take a nap on the couch. With a kid like Donovan it was hard to get a nap at all, but that late afternoon he tried to get fifteen minutes in before heating up one of the prepared dinners his cook had left for them. Usually most of Donovan's energy had been spent in the extensive afterschool program he was in and he was a little calmer by the time he got home.

That day Dai had high hopes for a little shut eye after dealing with a client who wanted to renegotiate their contract and another who wanted him to increase production.

He'd just managed to drift off to sleep only to be awakened by his son's panicked voice.

"Dad, Dad! Wake up! She's going to kill her. She's going to kill her!"

"What have I told you about TV shows?" he said in a groggy voice. "If you find it too scary turn it off."

"Please, Dad, please! You gotta help!"

Dai slowly opened his eyes. He yawned and stretched his arms. "What show are you watching?"

"You gotta do something!"

"How many times do I have to tell you that TV shows aren't real?"

"Please Dad help her." Donovan sounded near tears. Looked near them also.

That's when Dai noticed that the TV wasn't on but he still heard voices. Loud voices. And they both sounded familiar.

He quickly sat up. "What's going on?"

"Ms. Cardoza's gonna kill her."

Dai picked up the cell phone from where Donovan had dropped it on the floor. He couldn't see anything but the sky. "Elena? Elena!"

Someone picked up the cell phone and soon Cat's face appeared on the screen. She grinned and waved. "Hey guys."

"Hey, is Ava okay?"

She looked away then nodded and said, "She's great. You know she's a fighter. Dai, remember that maneuver you once showed her? She put it to good use. The way she—"

Ava appeared on the screen looking disheveled. "Ignore her," she said breathless. "Everything's fine. Just a misunderstanding."

Dai surged to his feet. "What happened?"

"I just told you."

"Don't play games with me, Ava. Is Elena there?"

"Not anymore."

Cat's face popped into the frame. "My sister made sure of that," she said with pride.

Ava pushed her away. "It's okay. Leave it."

"She might be coming for you next. So make sure your alarm is working."

Ava turned to her sister, who was now out of view, and said, "You're not helping."

"She looked mad. They should know in case—"

Ava looked at them and waved. "I've got to go."

Dai didn't want her to. "Are you sure you're okay?"

Ava flashed a mischievous grin that had him focusing on her lips in a way he never had before. "Of course," she said with a laugh. "Have you forgotten how we met?"

14

---

15 YEARS AGO

"GET HIM!"

Dai stood in the hallway waiting for a friend when he saw a guy in full American football gear from a rival school rush into the boy's locker room.

Three guys followed from a good distance behind him.

Moments later they came out. "Did you see anything?" one of them asked Dai, a guy tall enough to reach up and touch the ceiling if he wanted to. "Did you see someone come out here?"

He shook his head.

"You better not be lying," the guy next to the tall one said. He looked big enough to bench press a truck.

Dai held up his hands and shook his head once more. He wanted to get through his sophomore year without any trouble.

The three guys grumbled amongst themselves before they turned and left.

Dai was about to leave too, his friend was late and he'd gotten tired of waiting, but then noticed his shoelaces had become untied.

He'd been in a foul mood after losing a potential job. He

needed the extra money. While his mother made good money as a project manager at a local non-profit that tried to address technological disparities in low income and immigrant communities, finances could still be tight and he wanted to help out during what the news people kept calling a Recession. He could have gotten the job if he'd been a little more flexible when the interviewer had said, "Dai is a little hard to say, can I call you David?" Dai flatly said no.

He didn't get the job and wondered if he'd been too rash.

He was ruminating on what his temper had cost him when he'd noticed his shoelaces.

If he hadn't bent down to redo them he wouldn't have seen a female calmly walk out of the boy's locker room.

What struck him the most wasn't the fact that she was female, but that she was adorable. It wasn't a term he used lightly. Or really ever used at all. Especially not to describe the teenage girls who filled his high school.

But this girl was adorable, from her big brown eyes, round brown cheeks, black hair pulled back into a puff at the nape of her neck, that reminded him of licorice and cotton candy. Her pink colored jeans and matching earrings, made him think of a sweet shop and cartoon bunnies. He couldn't help but stare.

She didn't notice him as she walked past.

Dai stood to his full height and leaned against the wall, intrigued. He wasn't going to let her get away that easily. "So what do I get for pretending not to see that?"

She slowly turned and looked at him with such a cool, regal bearing he almost bowed. "Pretending not to see what?" she said. Even her voice sounded more modulated and mature than the other girls.

He blinked. Suddenly she wasn't as adorable as he'd first thought. Those big brown eyes held a sharp intellect that made him uncomfortable. He'd underestimated her.

She intimidated him and he didn't like feeling intimidated. He couldn't fight her with words, but there was another way. He cleared his throat. "Hey fellas!" he shouted in a sing songy voice.

She rushed over and covered his mouth. "What do you want?"

He pointed to the hand covering his mouth. She removed it. Luckily for her, the guys were out of hearing range, but she didn't need to know that. "A fair trade."

"What class are you failing?"

"Who says I'm failing a class?" Dai said offended.

"People are always asking me for tutoring lessons. Plus, I'm in two classes with you and you look half asleep most of the time."

"You're in my class?" He was certain he'd never seen her before. He would have remembered.

"Two classes. But I'm not surprised you didn't notice me. Someone like you wouldn't notice someone like me."

He felt insulted, even though she was right. Their class sizes weren't that big and to be in the same room twice, weekly, and not notice, didn't speak well of him. "Well, I—"

"What do you want?"

"I could use some help with history." He hadn't meant to say that. He didn't even know why he'd spoken to her in the first place, but there was just something about her that intrigued him even though he sensed it was best to stay away.

She could cut him down with a look or a word. He was no match for her.

She took a step back, folded her arms and shook her head. That was all the information he needed. She was turning him down. She started talking but he'd already zoned out. Besides, she was using words he didn't understand. Probably thought he was an idiot. That wasn't anything new.

When she finally stopped speaking he nodded and said, "See you around," then turned.

"Where are you going, dummy?"

He spun around. "Dummy?"

"Yes. I ask you a bunch of questions and you just nod and say 'See you around?' I thought you wanted me to help you."

"I do." He paused. "Wait, you will?"

She hung her head and sighed. "Oh my God, Dai."

His mouth fell open. "You know my name?"

Her head shot up and she sent him a look.

"Right, right," he quickly remembered, "we're in two classes together."

"Plus it's sort of hard not to notice a guy who at least three people are sketching in class because he's so good looking."

He felt his face heat.

"You know, if you ever need extra money you could be a live model. My sister Maya says they use them all the time at the college." She suddenly frowned. "But there's probably an age limit. So maybe in a couple of years."

Him? A model? No way. Jeans and a clean T-shirt were the only things keeping him from being a fashion disaster. "I wouldn't even know what to wear."

"You wouldn't have to wear anything."

He frowned. "I wouldn't?"

"I'm talking about being a nude model."

His face felt as if it was on fire.

She smiled and tilted her head like a mischievous sprite. "Wow. I didn't expect that. You're more innocent than you look." She looked suddenly thoughtful. "I guess we have something in common. I look innocent but you actually are. It's refreshing."

The smile frightened him. He liked it too much and yet he

couldn't figure her out. That was bad. He'd made a mistake. "I changed my mind. You don't—"

"I'll give you five sessions. At your house. Try anything and there will be blood." She paused, assessed him in one sweeping look, then laughed. "Never mind. You're not the type."

He didn't like her looking at him like he was some pathetic dweeb who'd never kissed a girl or was too shy and dumb to speak to a girl. Dai felt ready to tell her where to go when she said, "You're a gentleman."

"A gentleman?"

"Yep. A man of your word. And I owe you for keeping your mouth shut. So do we have a deal?"

She scared him a little and he liked it. But still wasn't sure.

She shocked him by making a loud buzzer sound. "Time's up. You lose. See you around." She turned.

He grabbed her shoulder and yanked her back with such force she crashed into him.

"I'm sorry," he said.

She rubbed her shoulder. "You don't know your own strength."

"Did I hurt you? I didn't mean it."

"It's okay."

"So...uh...you'll help me?"

She studied him for a moment. "You won't change your mind again?"

He shook his head.

"Good."

She was a few yards away when Dai remembered something important. "Wait, what's your name?"

"You'll figure it out."

It took some sleuthing but he eventually did: Ava Kayode.

15

Ava hadn't planned on getting caught. Especially not by a boy who had no qualms in blackmailing her. But Dai was known for getting into trouble. She wasn't. She had to keep him silent even if it meant adjusting her schedule to help him. His place was best. She didn't want anyone seeing them together.

She made him promise that no one would know about their arrangement. She had cultivated her reputation too well to have it sullied by someone who treated school as if it were a rec center.

Dai usually arrived late to class and when he did show up didn't seem remotely interested in anything. Except girls, mechanics-he seemed to have more car magazines than books—and jewelry. She didn't trust guys with six earrings and an onyx colored ring.

But she didn't regret her choice.

Until she stepped inside his apartment. She didn't know where to rest her eyes. She'd never seen so many protest posters.

"Uh," Dai said a little embarrassed after telling her to remove her shoes, "My mom has a passion."

And what a passion. The walls were filled with posters from San Francisco to Detroit to DC showing community rallies and civil rights conventions dating back to the eighties. It was so different than her own home where emotions were buried. She never could imagine speaking up like this. Having all her opinions and thoughts on full display. Being liked meant too much. Being accepted meant even more.

Her gaze shifted to pictures displayed on the bookshelf. She stopped at the picture of a light skinned black boy of about five wearing a Ghanaian smock.

"I didn't know you had a younger brother."

"I don't."

"This is you?"

He nodded.

She almost asked him what happened. How this adorable cherub grew up to look so mean. Or even how a little boy who looked more African in his youth could grow up and appear racially and ethnically ambiguous years later.

When she'd first seen Dai walk into the classroom, running his hand through his curly black hair before he slid his lean body into a seat then promptly fall half asleep, she'd thought he was from the Philippines or Samoa not the product of a Japanese-American mother and Ghanaian father.

She saw him in a more recent photo towering over his mother, an attractive, muscular woman dressed in athletic clothes, holding a volleyball, then looked back at his childhood photo.

"I hardly recognized you," she said. "Perhaps if you smiled..."

"I'm not going to smile."

"Aww but look at those cheeks. You were so cute."

"Some people still think I am."

"True." She turned away from the bookshelf. "So is it just us?"

"For now. My mother won't be home until late." He scratched his cheek, unsure. "Is that okay?"

Ava had to stop a smile. He really was sweeter than he looked. "That's fine."

An hour later she wanted to murder him.

She'd tutored before. She helped her sister and friends. But Dai proved a challenge. He couldn't seem to keep anything in his head. Not dates or names or anything. She felt her patience thinning.

They sat at the dining table. The only progress they'd made was through a bag of honey roasted peanuts and two cans of soda.

"Are you even trying?" Ava said.

"No, I'm not," Dai shot back. "I'm acting this stupid because I wanted to spend time alone with you so that you can look at me like I'm an idiot. It's a hobby of mine."

He looked as frustrated as she felt. She stood up. "Okay. Let's go for a walk."

THE APARTMENT COMPLEX sat on the corner of a main street and side road. They decided to head down the small tree lined side road that led to a row of houses.

They didn't talk until Dai eventually said, "So why were those guys chasing you?"

"Because I planned it that way."

When she didn't expand further he said, "And why was that?"

"They hurt a friend of mine. They thought it would be real

fun to lure him to the gym by pretending to be a girl he liked then strip him naked, take pictures and then post them. They found it hilarious. I didn't. So now our star running back thinks some guy from a rival school slimed the new Lexus he got for his birthday. But that's just the beginning. The other two will get what's coming to them soon."

Dai visibly shivered. "Remind me not to get on your bad side."

"You're smart. You won't."

Dai stared down at the pavement feeling his ears burn. Nobody had called him smart before and after their terrible tutoring session he hadn't proven otherwise, so he decided not to believe her. Even though what she'd said made him feel good.

"I noticed you had a lot of job applications on the kitchen counter."

"Yeah, just need some extra funds."

"Don't know if you'd be interested, but an uncle of mine owns a machine shop and might be able to use some help."

His eyes widened. "Really?"

"Sure. But...do you like cars?"

She'd meant to tease him since she knew cars were an obsession of his, but he didn't see the joke and answered with passion. "You can tell your uncle I would be one of the best hires he's ever had. I'm amazed by how mechanical energy can thrust something into motion. I know about cars and motorcycles and mopeds and—"

Ava laughed at his enthusiasm. "I'll let him know."

He placed a hand over his heart. "You don't know what it would mean to me."

"Because you really need the money?" she said trying to be delicate.

"No, like I said, the money's sort of extra. It's just—"

Dai rubbed the back of his neck. "It's something I know how to do. Everywhere else...I feel inadequate."

She nodded. "Okay. Tell me about a car engine."

"Which type? The internal combustion, hybrid or plug-in? And if I were to talk about internal combustion there's ongoing research to develop different types to help the environment like low temperature combustion that doesn't make the engine get as hot. But if we really wanted to talk about something incredible it'd be cars driving themselves."

"What?"

"It'll happen," he said then launched into the history of autonomous automobiles something she'd never heard of in all her school studies. He proceeded to tell her when cruise control was created; about the Stanford Cart a remote controlled TV-equipped robot that appeared in the 60s; the first autonomous passenger vehicle in the 70s, and then went on to talk about a remote piloted aircraft.

He then shared his admiration for Granville Woods, an African American inventor who patented parts for electric streetcars and a system for train stations and moving trains to communicate with each other by telegraph among dozens of other inventions.

Ava stopped walking and waved her hands before he got his second wind and started discussing the possible changes with public transportation.

"Wait, wait," she said. "You can remember all that but you can't remember the date for the Norman Conquest? Or the expansion of industry from 1868 to 1901?"

He smiled, sheepish. "I know. Things like that just won't stick in my head. It's like if I can't see it, it doesn't exist. With a machine it's there. In my mind's eye."

Ava clasped her hands together. "That's it!"

"What?"

She frantically looked around then grabbed his hand. "Quick we've got to run before they find us."

Dai stared at her confused. "Who?"

"I sabotaged that damn new construction. Got them good. See all this land? They want to put a railroad through it. Telling us about jobs and all that will happen to this town. But I don't buy it. People are getting rich. I'm just not sure it will be us."

And for the next several minutes, as they continued walking, she pretended to be a person who feared the new transportation that was encroaching on her land and changing the landscape. Then she had him pretend and visualize what it must have felt like. The smells, the sounds, the sights. Then she had him pretend to be an engineer and tell her all the possibilities and improvements that had happened and were bound to happen. Next, they were the railroad barons and saw things completely different.

And after an hour connecting Dai's interest of transportation technology with the role of big business in the late nineteenth to the early twentieth century, Dai finally understood and was able to answer her questions about the expansion of industry in America.

"You're crazy," Dai said but laughed pleased that he'd managed to get all her questions right. He hadn't even realized he was learning anything until he discovered how much he was able to recall. He didn't feel frustrated or stupid. She made learning fun.

And from that day they no longer studied in the traditional way. Ava got Dai moving (walking, sometimes jogging), and pretending—even using parts of a car engine to compare them to the seats of power in government. And she expanded her five sessions into ten allowing them to meet three times a week. And he started working at her uncle's mechanic's shop. (A man who wasn't a real uncle but a family friend.)

Life was great.

Then he broke his promise.

16

He hadn't meant to.

Promises were sacred. Dai always kept his word. His friends knew he was somebody they could trust. He didn't want to be like his father.

But that autumn day, Dai had been so shocked and surprised by how well he'd done on his history test that when he'd spotted Ava in the hall he'd called out her name.

She turned around and the alarm on her face (as well as the amazement on the faces of the two girls beside her) should have alerted him that something was wrong, but the joy he felt dulled his senses. He felt overjoyed to see her and tell her his good news. "I got a B," he shouted at her. "Can you believe it?"

She blinked slowly.

It was then he realized his mistake. How he'd stepped out of the high school hierarchy. She didn't want anyone to know she'd been tutoring him. Of course her reputation wouldn't be too damaged. Everyone would see him as a pity case for the popular Ava.

The weight of his embarrassment made the walls feel as if they were closing in on him; the people who had been rushing past so quickly before, seemed to move in slow motion.

He took a step back, suddenly feeling grimy and out of step with the judging eyes all around.

She walked over to him. And it felt like forever as the walls continued to close in and his heart raced. He started to sweat. He took another hasty step back, making a loud bang when he crashed against a locker. People turned to stare, giving him more attention he didn't want. He saw one of Ava's companions snicker.

"Sorry," he said quickly, hoping he could divert disaster. If she decided to give him a verbal tongue lashing he was no match and although he was bigger, there was no way he was touching her. "I know I shouldn't have—"

She threw her arms around him and hugged him. "I knew you could do it," she said.

He didn't move at first. Then he felt her pulling away and grabbed her before she could. He hugged her back filled with a sense of joy and relief. He felt as if he could fly. He lifted her up and spun her around. She laughed and he laughed with her.

As he set her on the ground he overheard someone say, "Are they dating?"

"No way," their companion said with authority, "Ava'd never date a guy like that."

"He's cute though."

Their voices faded but Dai didn't care what they said. Their words didn't bother him.

He knew he and Ava made a strange pair but as he looked into her sharp brown eyes and basked in the glow of her smile, in the pride she had in him, suddenly nothing else mattered. They were both in their own world. The world she'd opened up for him with their make-believe stories and scenarios. He'd never felt more himself than when he was with her.

"I've got to go," she said.

He nodded, suddenly not knowing what to do with his hands, awkwardly shoving them into his jeans' pockets then taking them out again, unsure what he should do or say next. Did he ask her to tutor him some more so he had a chance to see her again?

"I'll call you," she said.

And he nodded again, grateful she'd said something, since he'd lost the power of speech. Something that had never happened before. She waved goodbye and he waved back, watching her return to her friends.

"Another one of your charity cases," one of her friends said loud enough for Dai to hear.

The other one said, "Ava's so sweet she can't say no. She'll help anyone, won't you?"

Dai didn't hear Ava's reply, but guarded himself when she called him later that night.

At first he jumped when he saw her number on his cell phone. When she'd said she'd call he'd thought she was just being polite. Or that she'd wait a couple of days. He'd never imagined she'd reach out to him so soon.

"Aren't you going to answer it?" his mother asked him.

"Right." He picked up the phone and clumsily flipped it open, losing his grip. The phone did a somersault out of his hand and landed on the ground. He scrambled to pick it up but in his haste he ended up kicking it out of reach. He lunged to reach it but his mother swiftly snapped it up before he could and answered, "Hello? Who is this?"

"Give me the phone," he said in a desperate whisper.

"Oh, *Ava*. Yes, Dai's told me about you. I'm his mother. Sorry we haven't had a chance to meet yet. Hopefully I will soon. I can't thank you enough for all that you've done for him."

"Cut it out," he mouthed. But his mother just smiled. She was killing him and enjoying every minute of it.

"Dai? He's around here somewhere. Just give me a minute." She put the phone on mute and held it close to her chest. "She has a nice voice. I can see why you like her."

"It's not like that."

She sent him a look, doubtful. "Sure, sure." She held the phone out to him.

He snatched it from her and swallowed, annoyed by how happy and eager he was to talk to Ava. He took a deep breath then headed to his bedroom and closed the door before he hit unmute.

"Sorry I talked to you at school."

"You broke your promise," she said. "I've been trying to think of ways to punish you."

His heart fell. She didn't sound angry but he wasn't sure. "I know I messed up and—"

"So you'll have to be my friend."

"What?"

"That's your punishment."

He sat down on his bed confused. "How is that a punishment?"

"Won't your friends rib you for knowing someone like me?"

He thought for a moment then shook his head before he realized she couldn't see him and said, "No."

"You're lucky. I've already gotten an earful."

"And it doesn't bother you?"

She sighed. "I know it should, but I really don't care about them all that much. I have lots of friends but most of them aren't real."

"Oh."

"I think you'll be the first."

"Your first real friend?"

"Yes. Someone I actually like talking to. Someone I actually find interesting. I don't have to pretend with you, it's refreshing. I don't find you exhausting. I get to be me."

He switched the phone to his other ear relieved she could say what he felt. "Me too." He cleared his throat. "So we're cool now, right? I can talk to you when I see you at school?"

"Yes."

He tugged on his lower lip then said, "Will you still tutor me?"

"It can't be as frequent as before, but yes."

"And I can call you and we can hang out sometimes?"

"No."

"No?"

She laughed. "God Dai! Why are you being so serious? Of course you can. We're friends now. That's what friends do."

"But I've never had a friend like you before."

"Same here. So that's why I have two requests."

He braced himself. Here it comes. "Okay."

"First, always be yourself."

"Is that some sort of riddle?"

"No, I mean it. People sometimes change to impress me and I find it tedious."

He didn't know what "tedious" meant but it didn't sound good. "Sure, fine. I'll be myself. That's easy. What's the other request?"

"If being my friend gets too hard you'll let me know."

He couldn't imagine that ever being true. He shrugged and nodded then again remembered she wasn't in the room with him and said, "Okay."

"Knowing me might not be easy for you."

"Because I'll have to keep all your secrets and make sure I don't get on your bad side?"

"Something like that."

"Not a problem."

"One day it might be," she warned him.

That day came when he met her mother.

17

———

WHILE DAI's mother adored Ava from their very first meeting (she'd arrived home early from work one day, invited Ava to stay for dinner then spent the next two hours telling her about the rising technology disparities and how her nonprofit was fighting for change, one of the few traits she shared with her mother, a fifth generation Japanese-American, who was a prominent judge in Washington State, and to his relief Ava didn't look bored).

Her mother, on the other hand, didn't like him. At all.

Dai hadn't realized it at first when Ava invited him over that spring afternoon. Somehow he'd told her how generator's fascinated him and she told him her family had one and had invited him over to see it.

First he had to get over her neighborhood. It was a far cry from the apartment complex where he lived. Then he had to get over her house. It didn't look like a house to him, it looked like a mansion.

He knew she came from money but he didn't expect to

enter a house with ceilings as high as a cathedral's and furniture he was afraid to touch.

He started to take off his shoes, but she told him it was okay and led him to where the generator was.

She took him to the patio, where they sat at a table that could stretch the entire width of his apartment, and they chatted then she suddenly froze and swore. "I forgot what time it was. I'm so sorry."

Dai didn't understand her change in behavior or why she was apologizing to him until he heard a clicking sound.

He hadn't recognized them as high heels until Ava said, "It's my mother. Remember, just be yourself. I'll handle the rest."

The way she was speaking made him feel as if she was preparing him for battle.

In a way she was because the striking older woman dressed in a blue suit, a bright red scarf draped around her neck, who appeared in front of the sliding glass doors, was impressive.

"Who is this?" she said.

"My friend Dai," Ava said emphasizing the word friend. "Dai, my mother."

He nodded. "Nice to meet you, Mrs. Kayode. Thanks for having me."

"You're welcome," she said with such cool politeness that he hadn't realized he'd met an adversary.

She pointed to Ava then motioned her forward. "Come here."

"Right now?"

"Yes."

"Can't this wait?"

"No."

"But Mom—"

"I said come here."

Ava looked at Dai with regret. "Forgive me. I'll be right back. Wait here."

"Sure," he said, watching her go. He wasn't good at waiting. He got restless easily so after a few seconds he stood up and stretched. He sat back down and drummed a beat on the table, leaned forward and touched the tips of his fingers together in a rhythmic pattern, sat back again. Stood up. Sat down. Scratched his cheek. Rubbed his nose.

It was then he noticed the scent of oranges. Why was he smelling oranges?

"You can't sit still can you?"

Dai jumped at the unexpected voice and turned to the plain faced girl whose long skinny brown arms and legs reminded him of Anansi. A trickster god who sometimes took the form of a spider in the tales his father used to tell him.

He couldn't believe she'd occupied the seat right next to him and he hadn't heard her.

"Sorry, didn't mean to scare you," she said before taking another sip of her large orange flavored ice. "I'm Cat."

"Dai."

A mischievous grin touched her lips. "I know. But I had to see for myself."

"See what?"

"The reason why Ava's in so much trouble." She waved a finger. "Ava never gets in trouble. Not really. She got a B minus once but that was quickly forgiven and relatively minor. So this is a first."

"She's in trouble because of me?"

Cat nodded then set her cup on the table. "In case you're curious, this is what's happening right now." Cat straightened her spine and took on her mother's tone and accent. "What are you doing? Why would you invite someone like that here?" Cat sent him a sideward look and said, "That would be you," before shifting back to her imitation. "Does our reputation and yours mean nothing to you?" She changed her voice to Ava's. "Yes, Mom."

"You have plenty of friends. You don't need one like that. Are you trying to be rebellious?"

"No, Mom."

"Do you want to disappoint us?"

"No, Mom."

"All that we've done for you and this is how you repay us? You have a long life ahead of you, but there are many potholes and people who can distract you from your desired path. I have nothing against him as a person. God's children come in many shapes and sizes. But you know who you associate with not only affects your reputation but also your behavior. You can pick up very bad habits from someone like that. Please consider how this affects all of us."

Cat sat back, picked up her drink and took a long swallow before she gazed up at the sky.

Dai stared at her alarmed by her sudden silence. "That's it? What does Ava say?"

Cat returned her gaze to him and shrugged in sympathy. "Sorry, that's as far as I can imagine. I've never seen Ava defy our mother before. Your days may be numbered." She patted him on the back. "I'm sorry but this might be for the best."

Dai blinked, amazed that Cat no longer looked as plain faced as she had only moments ago. She had kind eyes. Her words seemed genuine as did her concern. He didn't think he would like her but found that he did.

"I think I can win your mother over," he said. "Might take some time but..." His words trailed off when she shook her head.

"No, you can't and really it's not worth it. Better off to have another friend."

Tell me if it's too much being my friend. He remembered Ava telling him that. Now he understood.

He glanced up at her magnificent house. Their lives were so different. She had lots of friends, did well in school, her parents had money. His paternal grandfather had money, which his father spent quickly. A charmer, who'd come to the US to study, married Dai's mother and then had returned to Ghana when Dai was three because he hadn't matured enough to take on the responsibilities of being an adult and preferred to depend on his family's money.

His father would infrequently show up in their lives with lots of gifts, money (usually enough that would pay the rent for years) and entertaining stories before he would disappear from their lives again, for another two years or so. Dai loved his father but he'd learned not to trust him.

Trusting was hard for him. But he trusted Ava. They had different personalities. But it didn't matter. He liked knowing her. And he wasn't ready to give up on her.

"I don't want another friend," he said. When he turned he realized the Anansi girl had left as silently as she'd appeared.

18

HE HEARD the sliding glass doors open. "I'm so sorry about that," Ava said.

Dai jumped to his feet when he noticed she'd put on a jacket that she hadn't had on before and her eyes were red. She looked like she'd been crying.

"Are you alright?"

"Yes." She rubbed her eyes embarrassed. "Sorry, I always cry when I get into trouble. I *hate* getting into trouble. Does it bother you? I'll be okay in a minute."

"No, I'm...should I go?" He hated the thought that he'd caused her pain somehow. He felt guilty. He didn't like being happy when she looked so miserable.

"Only if you want to."

"I don't."

She flashed a watery smile. "Good."

"But is there something I can do?"

"Yes." She looked around then whispered, "Follow me," before she ran to a large bush at the far end of the yard and ducked behind it.

Dai crouched in front of her. "What are we doing?"

Ava looked around again then pulled out a tied up cloth napkin from her jacket and placed it on the ground. "You're going to help me eat these petit fours Mom's been saving for herself." She untied the napkin and revealed ten tiny cakes.

"But won't you get into more trouble?"

"No, Cat said she'd take the blame." Ava popped one in her mouth then held another out to him. "Quick, before she looks for us."

Dai hastily shoved three in his mouth making her laugh. They quickly finished the stolen goods giggling their way through Ava's petty revenge against her mother.

Dai wiped his face to make sure he hadn't left evidence of their delicious crime. "What did you tell your mother about me?"

Ava took the napkin from the ground and shoved it in her jacket pocket. "I said you were my friend." She rose to her feet and headed back towards the house.

Dai followed her, silent for a few steps. He rubbed the back of his neck. "And she doesn't like that?"

"Nope."

"And you don't care?"

Ava paused, thoughtful. "I do." She nudged him with her elbow and smiled. "But not enough to stop being friends with you." She glanced up at the house and waved.

Dai followed her gaze and saw Mrs. Kayode frowning down at them from the second story window. He nodded in acknowledgement. Her frown increased before she spun away. He remembered the sight of her red scarf slapping against the window before she disappeared.

"I'm glad you stayed," Ava said. "I wasn't sure you would. That's why I sent Cat to keep an eye on you."

"You didn't have to do that." He slid an arm around her

shoulders and gave her a friendly squeeze. "I wasn't going anywhere."

"Never hurts to make sure," she said then flashed a devilish grin that hadn't changed in fifteen years.

They'd been inseparable since that day. People had been certain they'd lose touch when Ava went away to college in Delaware. He couldn't blame her for choosing a college out of state and having a chance to free herself from her mother's gaze.

He'd been a little worried that she'd outgrow him. That she'd meet people who were far more interesting than he was, a guy who decided to continue working at the machine shop instead of going to university like her. But he needn't have been worried. The miles couldn't break their bond.

When she hosted a small get together to celebrate her first job (a catered affair where hardly anyone spoke to him) he overheard one of her friends say, "I can't believe she's still friends with him."

But he wasn't as surprised as they seemed to be. By then, he saw them as best friends for life.

When he'd started losing his hair in his early twenties and felt insecure about it, Ava had encouraged him to shave his head, telling him he'd look sexy. He never felt he needed to choose to be one thing or another with her.

She accepted him completely and helped him to accept himself. She encouraged his business ideas, sharing what knowledge she'd gained from her parents. She was the one who made sure he never signed a deal where an employer had the rights to his side projects, which turned out to be a lucrative decision when he licensed some mechanical designs he'd come up with. She helped him when he stumbled; got him through bad break ups and his failed marriage.

He could trust her to be there.

Dai thought of that as he checked in on Donovan to make sure his son had fallen asleep. He'd been really anxious after Ava's phone call and it had taken some effort to calm him down.

He'd had to calm down too. He knew Ava could take care of herself but knowing she'd gotten attacked because of him...

Dai partially closed his son's door then crept down the stairs.

An aching loneliness seized him. Ava. He wished Ava was here.

He'd seen her only a few hours ago and yet he missed her. He had to resist the urge to call her and make sure she was alright. He knew she was.

But *he* wasn't.

He stopped in the foyer and stared down at her slippers. He rubbed his chest as if his need to see her, to have her there with him, had become a deep physical pain. What was wrong with him? He'd never felt this way before.

But something had changed when he kissed the back of her hand the other night. At first, as he helplessly watched her tears fall, he felt relieved she wasn't getting married. He felt glad Folu was out of the picture and a fierce possessiveness gripped him. He'd make sure Folu never came back in.

He'd never been jealous before.

But she was special to him. He knew how hard it had been for her to tell him the truth about Elena.

And now Elena had attacked her and—

His phone alerted him to a text. He went into the living room and grabbed it off of the coffee table where he'd left it.

Ava: Is Donovan okay?

Dai sat down on the couch, the pain in his chest easing, and grinned.

> Dai: Yes, I finally got him to sleep.

> Ava: I hope you're not still worried about me.

> Dai: I'm traumatized. I wish you were here. I wish I could make sure you were truly okay and that you'd spend the night so I could make you curry for breakfast and

Dai paused took a deep breath and erased his message. He started again.

> Dai: I'm not.

> Ava: Liar. I know you feel guilty. It felt good to hit her. Once for Donovan and once for you.

> Dai: Laughing emoji. That's my girl.

> Ava: Now go to sleep.

> Dai: Still can't.

> Ava: Me neither. Let's watch something together.

Dai leaned back and sighed in contentment. This is just what he needed. He turned on the flat screen.

> Dai: What do you have in mind?

He bit his lip, hesitated, texting was nice but he wanted to hear her voice. *Call and let me know.*
Silence.

> Dai: It's okay if you don't.

Silence.

Dai: Still there?

Ava: You want to see me don't you?

She knew him too well.

Dai: It'd be nice.

Ava: Fine. Let me wash off my face mask otherwise I'll give you nightmares. You choose the movie and I'll link to my webcam and turn my mic on. See you in five minutes.

Because she knew him so well, she popped up as a box on his screen in three.

And two hours later, as he drifted off to sleep, he couldn't recall the movie, but he could recall every time she smiled.

19

FOLU ALWAYS LOOKED best by candlelight.

Dinner had been his idea. Or at least Ava let him think so. She'd been carefully planning this seduction for weeks. She'd stayed away, carefully regained his trust, said what he wanted to hear, did what he needed, and made him feel confident.

The candlelight brushed his beautiful lips as he enjoyed one of his favorite dishes: spicy grilled shrimp. His brown eyes lit with pleasure when he looked at her across his dining room table.

There was every reason to marry this man. He was attractive, sweet, caring. He'd make a good husband. Her family would approve, they were compatible.

Ava smiled in response. Victory was close. With a few gentle nudges he would be hers again.

But she didn't want to marry him anymore.

That realization shook her.

It was devastating. She felt lost, unmoored. Who would she be if she truly allowed this broken engagement to be revealed? What would happen to all her careful plans?

But a part of her, the one she kept hidden, the one she only let a few people see, didn't care.

She didn't love this man. She barely liked him if she were truthful. He was decent enough. But all her feelings about him had been manufactured. She'd noticed his good looks, his suitable background, his acceptable manners before she even considered the man himself.

She had used him. He had a right to be afraid of her. That truth hurt the most. Somehow he'd seen past her façade and found her greatest flaw.

It wasn't that he was weak and she was strong. It was that he was honest and she was not. *Aren't you tired of living to other people's expectations?* She'd never allowed herself to consider a question like that. Had never been bold enough.

If only Dai hadn't...

She'd told herself she wouldn't think about that day.

The day Donovan had been over at a friend's house and Dai had asked her to come over and help him pack up Elena's things. Elena wanted to stop by and do it herself, but Dai hadn't wanted her in the house. But he didn't trust himself to do it himself either. "I'll probably break everything on purpose," he'd said.

So Ava came over and helped him untangle his life with the woman he'd once hoped to marry. The kitchen had been easy, the bathroom more intimate. But the bedroom. The bedroom had been difficult.

Not so much the picture of them on the bedside table, or the perfume on the dresser, or the clothes in the closet. But how much the room had changed. It didn't look like Dai anymore.

He wasn't one to go for light pastel colors. He liked deep red, purple, green hues. The abstract art was nothing like the stark black and white photos of cityscapes that used to hang there. One she'd liked was of a bridge, in stark contrast with dots of yellow lights, that would later glow in the dark. Others would find it tacky. She'd thought it was beautiful.

But it had been removed. There hadn't been a blending of lives. Elena had slowly taken over. Carefully, cleverly.

Ava sat on the bed ashamed. She lowered her head and sighed but lifted it when she heard a knock on the door.

Dai peeked his head in. "Are you finished yet?"

"You broke your promise."

He stepped into the room. "I did?"

"You promised not to change who you are." She gestured to their surroundings. "This isn't you at all."

He opened his mouth to deny it then sighed, a look of sad vulnerability crossing his face. "I really did love her. I wanted to compromise."

"This isn't a compromise."

Dai sat down beside her. "I'm tired of being single. I want to get married again. I'm ready to settle down and get it right the second time."

Ava took his hand. "You will, but not like this. We have to take the pictures down."

He gestured to one. "I hated that one the most."

"I'm not surprised since it's the picture of her vulva."

He turned sharply to her. "What?"

"Yes, some people take pictures of their genitals and then commission an artist to turn it into artwork. Does it look familiar now?"

He stared at the image open-mouthed. "Not in those dimensions." He frowned at her. "You're making this up."

"I'm not. I can outline it for you if you want."

"No."

"It's very well done."

He jumped up and took the picture off the wall and turned it the other way.

Ava pointed to the other picture. "You might want to take that one down too, since that's you."

His face flushed and he quickly removed it.

Ava walked up and rested a hand on his shoulder. "Bet you thought it was an abstract painting of a snake between two lemons."

"Shut up."

"An aubergine and two apples."

He turned to her. "You think I'm an idiot."

"I know you're not. I wouldn't have suspected anything either, if I hadn't known she'd gotten her lips done."

Dai blinked, surprised. "She's had plastic surgery? I saw a picture of her as a teenager and she didn't look all that different to me."

"No," Ava said slowly. "I'm not talking about her face. I'm talking..." She motioned to her waist. "Down there."

He stared at her blank.

She affectionately patted his cheek. "Still so innocent."

He tweaked her nose. "What are you talking about?"

"Labiaplasty, reshaping the labias or lips of the vagina."

"And you know this because...?"

"She told me."

His mouth fell open. "Really?"

"Yes."

"This is what women talk about with each other? I mean, how do you even start?"

"I needed a recommendation. Since I noticed she takes good care of her body, I asked if she knew any vaginal surgeons—"

Dai held up his arms in the shape of an X. "We're best friends but I don't want to know this. Especially if you wanted to do it for Folu—"

Ava fluttered her lashes. "You almost sounded jealous."

He pressed her lips together. "Say no more."

She swatted his hand away. "Let me finish. It wasn't for me. I needed the information for an acquaintance that'd undergone a brutal procedure in her youth. Unfortunately, the doctor Elena referred me to was better known for cosmetic improvements like appearance and size than the complex reconstruction my friend would need, so I couldn't use him. However, I couldn't help but remember her raving about him and how the surgery had changed her life. How pleased she was with the work he did."

Dai rested his hands on his hips and groaned. "I can't believe I've been staring at a large vagina all this time."

Ava walked over to the picture. "Technically it's a vulva because—"

"Leave it alone."

She glanced at him over her shoulder. "I just wanted to make sure."

"You don't need to."

"Okay, I won't." She faced him, folded her arms then slowly started to smile.

Dai narrowed his eyes.

Ava bit her lip.

He pointed at her in warning. "Don't."

Ava covered her mouth with both hands.

He took a menacing step forward. "I mean it."

She threw her head back and laughed.

Dai spun her around, tackled her to the bed and covered her mouth with his hand. "I'm serious. It's not funny."

Ava nodded, *Yes it is*, her eyes tearing up with amusement.

"No, it's not. It's embarrassing."

She removed his hand. "I'll take the one of you for safe-keeping."

Dai opened his mouth to respond, but couldn't think of

anything to say and collapsed on top of her, burying his face in the bed. He groaned again. "Just kill me now. You look after Donovan for me."

Ava patted him on the back. "There, there. Everything will be okay. Has anyone else been in your room recently?"

"No."

"Then your secret is safe with me."

He turned to her. "They always are."

Their bodies had been close before. She'd hugged him many times, held him, she knew the touch of his skin, the scent of his soap, the warmth of his breath.

But this time, with their noses almost touching, a sensuous fissure of awareness swept through her. She noticed the once teasing gleam in his gaze had become as soft as a caress. The weight of his body before would have been something she wanted to push away, but briefly, dangerously, she wanted to hold him and have him embrace her in return.

Not as friends.

She wanted to surrender to the wicked delight she felt now that Elena was gone. A woman who had never liked her, someone Ava could never please. Someone she knew was bound to try to separate Dai from her.

But now that threat was over.

She wouldn't lose him.

"Ava," Dai said, his voice a soft command, stirring something deep within her, beckoning her to him.

He'd said her name thousands of times before. But she'd never enjoyed the sound of her name on his lips like this. She'd never watched the shape and movement of his mouth as it formed the vowels and consonant.

He made the sound of her name feel like a whispered promise. *I am here for you. All that you need is right here.*

Or perhaps it was all her imagination.

Ava glanced up at the ceiling determined not to close her eyes even though she wanted to. "You weight a ton," she said, but didn't move, not trusting herself to touch him in case her body betrayed her and held onto him instead of letting him go.

Dai rolled onto his back and stared up at the ceiling too. "It's your fault for laughing at me."

"I wasn't laughing at you."

"Ava—"

She squeezed her eyes shut. Oh God that sweet sound again and he had no idea what he was doing to her. Because it didn't make sense. She wasn't supposed to feel this way. She sat up and cut off his words with a brisk, "You'd better go, I'll finish up here."

He didn't move.

She nudged him. "Go."

He held out his hand.

She took it and pulled him into a sitting position. "Now go."

He reluctantly stood, kissed her on the forehead. "Thanks for the help."

Weeks later she still felt the kiss.

Folu had kissed her, tenderly on the cheek. It hadn't left an impression. It had felt as pleasant and unremarkable as all the others.

She understood Elena's rationale. She would never have gone to the same extremes, but Ava understood the other woman's desperation. She'd felt it too when Folu broke off their engagement. So much of her future had been tied to this man. But manipulating him wasn't the answer. She didn't like who she'd become trying to please everyone else.

Folu deserved better than someone who felt like a fraud.

It had been weeks since Gwen's wedding. Weeks since Folu tearfully told her he couldn't marry her.

All was right in her world. Maya was helping Keeden with a major art project, effectively smoothing over relations between the Adesinas and Kayodes (although only Ava and Cat knew Maya was really using the project as a chance to get close to Keeden's best friend Bryant, which worried them a little). Melody hadn't bothered her again about what she'd overheard and work remained the same—neither tedious nor thrilling.

Her life was good.

People still thought they were getting married just as she'd planned it.

And she'd smiled her way through lies that had become exhausting.

"This will be our final dinner together like this," she said. "I'm ready to tell the truth."

Folu set down his utensils. "About that. I might have been hasty. You were right—"

"No, I wasn't. Let's not argue about this. I'll take the blame."

SHE WASN'T sure how to broach the subject until her mother gave her an opening one late afternoon.

"Where is my dear Folu?" her mother said, catching Ava in the kitchen finishing a mandarin. "I want to see him. It's been too long. How is he doing?"

"He's fine."

"You haven't invited him over in quite some time."

"I've been busy."

"Yes, I know," her mother said with a sniff. "Thank you for visiting your sister and making sure she wasn't making trouble."

Looking after Maya would have been a good excuse.

Visiting Maya at Keeden's house had taken time out of her schedule and been well worth it.

Her sister looked happier than Ava had ever seen her before. She wondered if she'd be able to claim that kind of happiness for herself one day.

If she wanted a different future, she had to take a little bit of Maya's courage. She had to stop stalling and tell her mother the truth. "We're no longer engaged."

Her mother put water in a kettle. She set the kettle on the stove.

"Did you hear me?"

She turned the stove on.

"Then I will repeat it."

Her mother spun around, her eyes flashed. "No, you won't."

Ava took a deep breath. "Folu and I are no longer engaged. We're not getting married."

Her mother's gaze turned cold. "We'll see about that."

20

———

Ava had never been the subject of a family meeting/discussion/interrogation before. It was usually Maya, sometimes Cat, rarely Gwen but never Ava.

Until now.

Ava looked around the living room and felt a strange sense of surrealness as she looked at the semicircle of faces in front of her. She felt like a defendant going before the court.

She should have been scared, but she wasn't. She had never been the center of attention this way. Usually her mother's distress would terrify her but today she felt oddly calm. And it was because of Maya. Something had changed.

There was a certain beautiful fire that burned within her sister. Before, Maya tried to fit in a little, but now she didn't look as if she cared. She looked as if she wanted to be somewhere else. Perhaps *with* someone else. Ava didn't know if it was Keeden or Bryant, she hoped it was the former, but she was happy with whomever or whatever had made her look that way.

It made Ava even more certain that she didn't want to try to fix things with Folu.

She didn't want to win him back. She was free. It was unsettling but a chance. A chance to find out what true happiness was. She'd been going through the motions all her life.

Her gaze shifted to Maya again and she took courage from a certain glow of defiance she saw.

No, she couldn't be as reckless as Maya and risk a friendship that was precious to her, but she also wouldn't marry a man because she was expected to.

Their family, including her new brother-in-law, looked at her, each one, except Cat and Maya, offering her differing reasons why she was making a big mistake.

"Do you want to end up like Maya?" her mother said with a note of disgust her sister didn't deserve." Ava sent Maya a look of regret. Maya didn't blink. "You don't know what you're giving up."

Ava barely listened to the rest. She heard her mother chiding Maya to say something, Gwen responded and Ava imagined herself far away. She wondered how Dai was doing. If Donovan had stayed out of trouble this week.

That surprised her. There was someone she worried about letting down more than her parents. She looked at Maya and saw that look of "I don't care."

"Tell her what a mistake she's making," her mother demanded.

"I can't do that," Maya said. "I don't think she's making one."

Her sister Gwen spoke but it was like buzzing in her ear. Maya was giving her permission to free herself from the obligations that had been with her for so long.

The buzzing noise stopped.

She heard her mother breathe a sigh of relief and then say, "Yes, that," not knowing what had been said before. "Listen to your sister."

Ava felt a sudden calm engulf her as she clasped her hand in her lap. "Which one?"

"Gwen of course."

"But I think Maya understands me more."

"Maya knows nothing!"

But Ava knew that wasn't true and felt the weight of that lie when Maya stood and closed the distance between them. She felt the warmth of her sister's hands holding her own. Giving her strength. Giving her courage. "One thing she knows," Maya said, holding Ava's gaze, "is that your sister loves you and will support whatever decision you make. You don't have to live your life fulfilling everyone else's expectation of you."

There was little Ava could do when her mother lurched at Maya and hit her on the back of the head. "Get out! I want you to pack the rest of your things and never set foot in this house again!"

Ava and Cat jumped to their feet and shouted, "Mom, no!"

But Maya calmly said, "It's okay," although it wasn't. Ava felt guilty for Maya facing a punishment that should have been hers. Maya had always taken the physical and verbal attacks her mother never directed to her or her other sisters.

She watched Maya leave the room then slowly sank back in her chair. That was the price for disobedience. Being locked out.

The barrage began again. More buzzing in her ear. More complaints about Maya that only steeled Ava more.

She hated causing hurt, she hated being in trouble and she felt the gathering of tears but they did not shake her will. She felt anger that her mother had focused her rage at Maya instead of her.

She sensed the finality of what had happened after hearing the front door close. Maya didn't slam it but the lock engaging hit Ava like a bomb. It felt no different than when Maya had been forced out at nineteen. Ava remembered standing by the window and watching her sister drive away.

This time she didn't get a chance too. She only listened to the car engine rev up and then fade away.

The look of relief on her mother's face made Ava grip her hand into a fist. She could not understand why her mother had such bad feelings towards Maya.

Her mother met her eyes. "That one has always caused me pain." She placed a hand over her heart. "Will you do the same? Will you hurt me this way? We only want what's best for you."

Instead of feeling shame, Ava felt anger. The same anger when her mother had dismissed Dai years ago, and had told Ava they couldn't be friends. She knew how to get back at her.

She knew how she would use her tears.

She fell to her knees and wailed. "I'm so sorry. I know I'm a disgrace. I know how miserable I'm making you but please don't force me to marry him."

Her mother gasped. "What are you doing?"

Ava pounded her chest as she'd seen a woman do in one of her mother's dramas. "I have tried to change. I have prayed to God. I have meditated but I cannot do it." She lowered her head to the ground. "Oh how wretched I am. I should leave too instead of causing you shame. I've hurt you and Folu and his family. I don't deserve to live!" She fell forward, prostrating herself on the ground, and wailed some more.

"No, no, my dear," she heard her father say in alarm. "That's not it at all."

"This is all my fault."

"We won't force you to marry anyone you don't want."

"I'm so sorry."

"It's okay, my dear," her father said. "Never mind."

Ava surged to her feet, covering her eyes. "I'm still so sorry," she said before she ran out of the room.

The worst was over.

For the first time Ava actually felt truly free. She'd planned her life so much around Folu she hadn't thought much about her own needs. She could now schedule anything—dinner with friends, a trip—on a whim without considering his needs. She didn't have to pretend to enjoy his mother's singing or his father's endless discussion about his coin collection.

Someone knocked on the door.

Ava hesitated before she cautiously said, "Who is it?" Her tears had long since dried so she needed to know if she had to get the waterworks started again.

"It's me," Cat said.

Ava fell back on her bed, relieved. "Come in."

Cat walked into the room with a grin. She closed the door and lightly clapped her hands. "That performance was amazing. I'm so proud of you."

Ava sat up and nodded in acknowledgement. "Thank you."

"Our parents don't know what to do now."

She chewed her lip. "Are they really upset?"

"Mom hasn't spoken for a full ten minutes."

"That is bad."

"But expected."

Ava sighed. "Still."

Cat pulled a snack bag from the pocket of her over long sweater. "It's not your fault you know. What happened to Maya."

"It still feels that way."

Cat sat down on the bed with a sigh. "I know." She chewed

on a chocolate stick. "She's better off. At least she's gotten over Bryant."

"How do you know that?"

"Know what?"

"That Maya's gotten over Bryant?"

Cat finished her chocolate stick and started on another. She shrugged. "Just a guess."

Ava sensed it was more than a guess. She knew her sister could be sly and secretive but Cat seemed even more so now. But Ava didn't get a chance to dig deeper when Cat said, "Why didn't you tell me about Folu first?"

Cat sounded hurt and she didn't blame her, they usually trusted each other. "I was trying to figure it out on my own."

"Because he's the one who wanted to back out and you had to take the blame?"

"How did you—never mind. I could have won him back but then realized I didn't want to."

"Does Dai know that?"

"What?"

"That you don't want to marry Folu anymore."

"No, I haven't told him. He's already got a lot on his mind. I doubt he'd care."

Cat sent her a knowing look and a sly grin touched her lips. "Oh, he cares. More than you think."

21

"Man, you're killing the mood more than the rain outside."

The rain had certainly put a damper on his cousin Koji's party but hadn't killed everything. There was still plenty of drinks, the rhythmic boom of hip hop music and raucous laughter that drifted through the stylish main room.

Koji sat on an armchair across from him, his girlfriend, Moriko, sat on the arm of the chair, and leaned against him. Her long black hair and ruby red lips reminded him of a vengeful ghost. Dai found her a little creepy but Koji adored her.

Dai finished his beer and set the bottle on the side table. "Sorry, I've got a lot on my mind."

Koji leaned forward, a curtain of black hair framing his face. He tucked a strand of hair behind his ear, revealing a dangling silver earring. "Is it Donovan?"

"In a way."

Koji's friend Letisha walked over to them, her silver fishnet stockings seeming to shimmer when she moved. An alluring contrast to her chestnut colored skin. She sat down next to Dai on the sofa. "Who did you leave the little hellion with tonight?"

"A friend." Thankfully Ava managed to fill in when his last babysitter quit and the one he could usually depend on was on vacation.

Koji stroked his goatee. "I didn't expect you to come alone."

"Me neither." Dai sighed. "We broke up."

His brows shot up. "You broke up with Ava?"

Dai shot him a look. "I wasn't dating Ava. I was dating Elena." He picked up the empty bottle, and stared at it before setting it back down. "Or at least I was."

"What happened?"

"This is not the place."

"Either tell me or put a smile on your face. You're killing the mood. I mean it. You've got that moody, gangster vibe going."

"But in a sexy way," Moriko said, her low, deep voice giving him goose bumps. Then she smiled, which made him want to run.

"You're making people nervous," Koji said.

Dai looked at his cousin. "What?"

"Relax."

Dai started to stand. He shouldn't have come. "Maybe I should go."

"No, you need another drink," Letisha said then left.

Koji pushed him back down. "No, no. Stay." He snapped his fingers. "I've got an idea." He lowered his voice. "I know someone who could make you forget all about Ava."

Moriko nodded. "Yes, forget her."

Dai gritted his teeth until his jaw ached. "For the last time, I'm not dating Ava. Never have. She's my best friend, that's all. It's Elena. E-len-a."

"Sorry, Ava, Elena whatever, this woman will make you forget all that. And she's free."

Dai stared at him stunned. "You think I need a prostitute?" He sent an uneasy glanced at Moriko. This was not the kind of conversation he wanted to have in front of Koji's girlfriend.

"No, no I meant that she's free tonight not that she's 'free' but you could think of it that way if you want. She likes you." He turned and scanned the crowd. "I think she's here somewhere."

"No."

Koji looked at him concerned. "You look stressed. Give yourself a little time alone and—"

"Thanks but no."

"So what happened?"

"Don't you have a party to get back to?"

"When you're miserable, I'm miserable."

Moriko crossed her legs. "And he's really miserable."

Dai shook his head. "I don't know why I came. I'm really not in the mood for this. I should go."

Koji's expression grew serious. "No. I will shut down this party in a heartbeat and send everybody home if you need me to. Tell me what's going on."

This was why he'd come. Koji was another person he could trust. But he wasn't going to tell him the truth. Not when others might overhear them. "We argued about Donovan. She wanted to handle him one way and I another and the worse part—"

"You were thinking of marrying her," Koji finished. "Because she was amazing and beautiful and got on with Donovan."

Dai sighed in regret. "Sometimes I talk too much."

"Thought she was a malicious witch," Moriko said.

Koji turned to her shocked. "You only met her twice."

"I knew from the first time. But I'm really sorry it didn't

work out," she added in her low voiced, creepy way, but her words sounded genuine.

"Thanks, I think."

Letisha returned with another beer and held it out to him. "What didn't work out?"

"He broke up with his girlfriend," Koji said.

Letisha gasped. "You broke up with Ava!"

Dai set the bottle down afraid he'd smash it. "What is wrong with you guys? Ava and I aren't dating. Have never dated. Will never date."

"Why not?"

"Because she's my best friend and that would be weird."

Koji ran a hand through his luxurious, black hair and Dai felt like yanking it, not because he was jealous, he'd gotten over that, but because he didn't want to talk about Ava. "And you've never thought about it?"

"No, it's not like that between us. Besides, she wants to marry someone else."

"So you *have* thought about it."

"No."

"He's right, though," Letisha added. "They would make a weird couple. I mean she looks sweet and adorable and he looks like he could make a body disappear."

"Thanks for that."

"I'm just being honest."

Koji shook his head. "Nah, you don't know Ava. Ava is something else. Personally, I think they'd make a great couple," Moriko said.

He blinked at her and she didn't look like a vengeful ghost anymore. He briefly felt like falling to his knees and thanking her as if she were a deity of good fortune. She was one of the few people who didn't think he and Ava were an odd pair. But of course she was wrong.

"We're not having this conversation," Dai finally said.

"Are you sure you don't want a little distraction?" Koji said.

Dai stood. These people were way to interested in his love life. "I'm good."

"Where are you going?" Koji said.

"You're right. I'm killing the mood. It's been an hour anyway and I want to give Ava a reprieve."

"You'd rather be with her than with us?" Koji said with a smile.

"Yes. No." He swore. "I told you it's not like that." Dai scowled. "Stop trying to mess with my head."

THE RAIN HAD STOPPED LEAVING the heavy scent of damp grass and mud as Dai walked to his car.

Of course he'd lied. Once, briefly, he'd thought of taking his relationship with Ava to another level. He'd missed her terribly when she'd gone off to college and when he'd seen her again after months apart, he couldn't believe how happy he'd been.

But then he was reintroduced to her world and realized how much he didn't fit into it.

"I can't believe she's still friends with him." The overheard comment still echoed because it revealed so much. First, that they were just friends, and second, anything more was out of the question.

He realized that her family wouldn't want her with someone like him. That he rarely got on with her other friends even though by twenty years old he'd already made a million from his various ideas and was on the path to make much more. Ava wanted someone who was a good conversationalist (to fit into her social circle) had a degree and could please her parents. He couldn't.

So he pushed that foolish thought away and sought to prove to himself that he was worth more, without realizing it. He met an attractive Chinese Jamaican lawyer, five years his senior, who liked his rough edges and gave him the confidence boost he needed; that he could be with someone with an advanced degree.

But soon, after a whirlwind romance and getting married, she realized Dai wasn't the man for her. While he considered himself a homebody, she thought he was boring.

He wasn't as mysterious and sexy as she'd first thought. Her dinner parties bored him, they didn't like the same movies. He needed action, she loved subtitles and talky independent movies and then there was Donovan.

Their son had been a difficult baby and even harder to handle as a toddler. The tensions started there and an already fragile relationship fell apart. Dai gained custody and she met someone else.

His relationship with Ava was perfect as it was. He wouldn't do anything to jeopardize that. Would he?

He remembered the night he kissed the back of her hand, how precious she'd been to him at that moment. He would have done anything to make her stop crying.

He hated her thinking she'd done anything wrong. That there was something wrong with her, when she was perfect. Perfect for the right man.

But he hadn't been thinking about that when he'd nearly crossed the line when she'd come to help him clear out Elena's things.

He'd only meant to make her stop laughing. He'd tackled her before. It had never been a big deal. But this time he almost kissed her.

His best friend.

Who still wanted to win back her ex.

22

———

Two GUILTY FACES looked up at him when Dai walked into the living room.

"Look out!" one of the cartoon characters on the flat screen said to another.

Ava scrambled to her feet, leaving behind the half-finished 3D puzzle she'd been helping Donovan with. "You're back early."

"Hmm." Dai sat on the couch. Donovan watched him, Ava rubbed her hands together. He knew the reason for their uneasiness. It was past Donovan's bedtime and Dai was usually strict about that. But tonight he didn't care, but also wasn't in the mood to let them know it.

"Did you eat anything?" Ava asked him.

Donovan pumped his fist in the air. "We got egg rolls!"

Ava headed to the kitchen. "I'll heat some up for you."

Dai grunted in response.

It felt good to be home. To be here. He sank deeper into the seat cushion and let out a sigh of relief. He didn't have to think for awhile.

He'd eat, put Donovan to bed, watch something until late and then head to bed himself. No worries. No cares. A simple, easy goal.

Donovan rushed over to him, jumped on the couch and siddled up close to him. "You're not mad, right? 'Cause it was my idea." He patted his chest. "Sandy didn't do anything wrong. I forced her."

"It's okay. I'm not mad."

Donovan sighed in relief. "I'm glad because she's so happy. She won't tell me why, but I can tell. This has been the best night ever."

Donovan then began to tell him about his day, but Dai barely listened. Ava was happy? What was she happy about?

Ava returned with a plate, knowing he didn't like using a tray, and sat down beside him with a plate of her own.

He shouldn't have watched her, but his son was right, she did seem happy. More carefree than before. Something had changed. She looked radiant and his food grew cold as he watched her pour duck sauce on the tip of the egg roll and slowly suck it off.

Once.

Twice.

He'd seen her do it thousands of times. Usually it would drive him nuts. Eat the damn egg roll already! He liked to tease her that he should just buy her a duck sauce flavored lollipop.

But this time he noticed the shape of her lips, how her mouth wrapped around the egg roll, sliding it halfway in before steadily sliding it back out again, with a nice firm pressure that was not too hard so the surface of the golden crust didn't break. He swallowed while his lingering gaze followed the path of her tongue as she licked her bottom lip in a slow swirl.

She added more duck sauce and sucked it off again. He felt his mouth go dry and his body grow hard.

He tore his eyes away and stared at the TV taking a big bite of his own egg roll. What the hell was wrong with him? It was Koji's fault. He'd planted dumb ideas in his head about him and Ava.

He didn't want that with her and he'd just broken up with Ava. No Elena! His ex's name was Elena!

Dai silently swore and mentally shook his head. Ava was his best friend.

That was all.

He'd always found her attractive. That had never been a problem and she was smart and funny and he liked her company and she made him laugh. He could trust her. Even when she annoyed him, like now, when she kept applying duck sauce until there was nothing left in the packet, and sucking it off, burying whatever flavor the egg roll truly had, knowing she could get more because he always kept extra jars just for her.

She looked satisfied, pleasured. Like a woman who'd gotten what she'd wanted... Then he remembered the feel of her body underneath him when he'd tackled her on the bed.

Agitated movement in the corner of his eye broke through his thoughts. He turned to see Donovan looking at him in a curious way. That was never a good thing. Especially when his son's gaze dipped to the front of Dai's jeans with an expression of puzzlement.

"Hey Dad. How come you—"

Dai shifted in his seat, wishing for the first time he liked using a lap tray. "Let it go, Dynamo." *Please. For your Dad's sake. Just this once, do as I say.*

Ava could not know what was going on. This was worse than having an abstract picture of a vagina in his bedroom. Ava would never let him forget it.

"But Dad."

Dai hardened his tone. "I mean it." He sent his son a dark

look, and saw a brief look of fear, which he regretted but knew he had no choice. He was in a fight for survival. He had to stop any questions.

Donovan jumped off the couch uncertain. "All right," he said, making Dai feel guilty.

Ava saved him from having to apologize by standing up and holding out her hand to Donovan. "Let your Dad finish eating and help me clean up the dishes."

Donovan took her hand and followed her into the kitchen saying, "But how come Dad's face is all red now?"

Dai groaned.

He didn't hear Ava's response and wasn't sure he wanted to.

Dai picked up his egg roll then set it back down. He couldn't sit still imaging all the questions Donovan was likely asking her. He didn't want them alone together.

He dashed into the kitchen, stood behind the island, since he hadn't completely gotten himself under control, and set his plate down.

So hard that it snapped in half.

Donovan flinched and hugged Ava, staring up at him with wide eyes.

Dai swore. "I'm sorry."

"I'm going to go to bed right away," Donovan said, running towards the door.

Dai called after him. "No, you don't have to—"

"Don't forget to brush your teeth," Ava said.

Dai briefly covered his eyes. He'd scared his kid. That was the last thing he wanted to do.

"What happened at the party?" Ava said.

He let his hand fall to his side. "Nothing."

She pointed to the broken plate. "You call this 'nothing'?"

He set the remaining egg roll aside on a napkin, it was still edible, then grabbed the trash bin. "I'm sorry." He started to use his arm to sweep the remainder of the food and the broken plate off the island into the trash bin.

"Stop," Ava said, grabbing his arm. "You could cut yourself."

He smiled, amused, easily pulling his arm free. "I won't cut myself."

"Let me get a small broom and dust pan." She pointed at him. "Move away from the counter."

He sniffed. "Or what?" he said, scooping the items into the trash with his hand. "You'll ground me?"

He washed his hands then grabbed a sponge and cleaned the counter.

She watched him. "What happened?"

"I told you. Nothing happened."

"You only took one bite." She held up her forefinger for emphasis. "One bite. By a man who could inhale an entire buffet and—"

"Hey."

"—And then you break a plate, not to mention you came home hours before I expected you to, and you're going to tell me nothing happened at the party?"

He set the sponge down. "Yep."

Her expression changed from curious to concerned. She took a step towards him. "Are you okay? Did you return early because you're not feeling well?"

The last thing he wanted her to do was touch him. Dai moved out of reach before she could touch his forehead or neck and check for a fever. "No, I'm fine." He rubbed his head. "Sorry about the food."

"It's okay." Ava hesitated then folded her arms. "I won't judge you, you know that. You can trust me. Do you want to talk about what happened in the living room?"

Oh hell no. He'd rather stab himself in the eye.

"Because I understand."

I'm just going to look at you and pretend we're not having this conversation.

"It's only human."

Still not going to say anything.

Ava sighed. "I know how you feel."

No you don't.

"You think it's too soon but it's not. Parties are places to meet other people. Tell me about her."

"Who?" Dai said, shock forcing him to break his vow of silence.

"The woman you met tonight." She grinned. "You were thinking about her." She waved her hand. "I won't tease you, so you don't have to pretend. I know what you were thinking. You were looking at me but you got this faraway look on your face and then..." She motioned her finger upward and released a high pitched whistle, miming a rocket launch.

Kill me now.

She thought he'd been fantasizing about somebody else. Part of him was relieved, another insulted. He'd been looking *right at her.* She was usually smart, but could be clueless to her sex appeal sometimes. That was Folu's fault and every man who had come before him.

But he couldn't tell her the truth and risk their friendship.

"Hmm."

"Did you get a number?"

"I'd rather not talk about it."

"Don't worry about what happened. We both know Donovan is not one to hold back what he sees." She lowered her voice. "One time he caught me doing this sort of dance routine and he asked me why my breasts jiggled."

Dai's gaze dipped to her chest then back to her face. He cleared his throat feeling his face grow hot again.

Kill me now and bury me deep.

"You were supposed to go and relax. Instead you come back looking more miserable than ever."

She on the other hand looked radiant.

"Must have been hard going to the party alone," she said. He knew she was trying to get him to open up, they usually talked about everything, but this time he didn't plan to say anything, no matter how hard she tried.

"Hmm."

"It's okay to admit that you miss her. You did love her."

He blinked. "You think I fell in love with someone I just met?"

"No, I meant Elena."

He flinched as if she'd struck him. "No. I don't miss her. Really, there's nothing wrong. I just didn't feel in the mood to party and...I'm sorry about what happened with the plate and my..." He waved his hand not knowing how to put it into words.

"Erection."

Yep, leave it to Ava to say it plain.

He nodded.

"It's fine. Let's talk about something else.

He ran a hand down his face. *Yes. Please. At last. Thank you!!*

"I've got news."

His heart started to race. She had something to tell him. Something that made her glow. She'd won Folu back and he didn't want to hear it. Not tonight.

Dai pushed himself from the counter. "It's too quiet. Let me make sure Donovan's really in bed. It might take a while if he's not so you don't have to stick around. We'll talk tomorrow." He turned and left the kitchen before she could reply.

23

———

Donovan wasn't asleep. He'd brushed his teeth and changed into his pajamas but laid in bed, staring up at him in a funny way. Dai tried his best to ignore his son's gaze as he tucked him into bed.

"Dad?"

"Yeah."

"How come your face got red with Sandy?"

"I don't know."

"Did she make you angry? Your face usually gets red when you're angry. Remember when Elena tossed away one of your sketches?" He'd drafted an idea on a napkin, which she'd mistaken for trash.

"That was one time and she apologized."

"Your face was so red."

He believed him. It hadn't been a good day.

"And then when she showed up unannounced and confused Nana for your housekeeper and had her cleaning the bathtub."

That had been an honest mistake and he still hadn't

forgiven his mother for tricking her like that. The reason he'd gotten angry was that Elena had criticized his mother for not dressing better. When he'd told Ava she'd laughed until tears ran down her cheeks. Then his mother had the gall to invite her over and retell the story and the two women had a good laugh at his expense.

"And then when she—"

"You make it sound as if I was always angry with her," Dai said. "I wasn't. I really liked her."

"You sure you weren't angry with Sandy?"

"I'm sure."

"Is it because she let me stay up later than usual?"

Was it wrong to imagine lifting the bed sheets until they covered his son's mouth and tucking in the sides so tight that he couldn't speak? "I told you I wasn't upset. It's been a long day. I'm tired. Sometimes my face gets red when I'm tired."

"Is that why your voice was different too?"

He rubbed the back of his neck. "Yes."

"Because it was never that way when you were with—"

"Drop it, Dynamo."

Donovan sighed, looked anxious. He wanted to say more but was trying not to.

Dai hung his head in surrender. "Okay, you can ask me one more thing."

"You and Sandy. You'll always stay friends, right?"

He looked at him surprised. "Why would you ask that?"

Donovan lowered his voice. "Tonight I heard her talking to Aunty Cat about Uncle Folu—"

Nope. Didn't care. Didn't want to hear it. "We've been over this. You know she's not my girlfriend."

"I know. But friends can still break up. I know."

Yes, he'd had a best friend in the first grade who'd later dropped him to be with other kids and the pain still stung.

Fortunately, Donovan had managed to find a new friend but the memory of the falling out hadn't left him.

It was why Dai was very careful who he introduced his son to. He'd dated quietly but Elena had been the first he'd allowed close to Donovan and in his life.

What a colossal mistake.

"We're not going to break up. Why would you worry about that?"

He shrugged.

Dai knew he was hiding something. But this was why he couldn't risk anything with his relationship with Ava. Donovan would be hurt the most.

"What's going on?"

"Nothing."

"Why are you worried about Auntie?"

He chewed his lip. "Because I love her."

"I know you do. She's not going anywhere."

"So you promise you're not angry about tonight?"

Dai kissed him on the forehead. "I promise."

SHE WASN'T SUPPOSED to still be here. She was supposed to have gone home so he could be alone.

But instead, Ava stood when she saw Dai walk into the living room.

"He's okay?" she said.

"He's fine."

"Now about my news."

"Ava—"

She held up her hands. "Don't worry. I know you're tired and this won't take long, but I have to tell you."

He still didn't want to hear it. He knew that made him a

bad friend but tonight he didn't care. He didn't want to see her, didn't want to smell her perfume, hear her voice, as she told him how she'd won Folu back. Perhaps she'd even tell him that they'd get married sooner than they'd planned. "Fine, tell me in the kitchen."

He had to do something else while she spoke. So in the kitchen he noticed the pile of mail, which looked larger than he'd expected it to be, on the table and flipped through it. He heard the words Folu (no surprise there) dinner (uh huh that's probably how she seduced him) mother speechless (that was rare but he supposed she was exaggerating for dramatic effect) Maya, house and something about a Nollywood drama but...

He stopped at the sight of a large manila envelope.

"Are you listening to me?"

Dai heard Ava's annoyance but couldn't even form the words to reply.

He grabbed the front of his shirt as dread gripped him. This envelope was the purveyor of disaster. He'd forgotten all about it. How could he have done this? It was almost the end of the school year. How could he have forgotten that?

"Are you okay?"

He ripped the envelope open. The words looked so innocent but their power poked all that he feared. *Thank you for your interest.*

Blah, blah, blah.

We are sorry to inform you...

"What's wrong?" Ava took the letter from his shaking hand. "What's that?"

Dai returned to the living room like a zombie and sunk into the sofa, holding onto the yellow sticky note that had been attached to the rejection. "The reason I'm going to have to beg Elena to take me back."

24

Ava placed the rest of the material that had come with the manila envelope on the coffee table. "You don't mean that."

Dai placed the note on top of them. "You're right. I won't need to beg. I'll sleep with her and pretend that all is forgiven—"

"You're not going to do that either."

"The school year's ending."

"So?"

"Summer break starts soon." He pointed to the letter. "I will do whatever it takes to get Donovan in this program."

He had to get him in. Last summer had been a disaster, three day camps, two hospital visits, one thousand dollars paid to a relative who'd agreed to look after Donovan but had left him without supervision.

He'd tried to get into the Boulders and Bridges summer camp since early winter, now if he didn't, he would be facing another stressful summer. Many places didn't know how to handle a kid like Donovan. And Elena had supported him in getting his son into this camp and Donovan had been so excited with the possibility.

He knew parents had to meet a rigorous criterion, prove they were there for their kids, be active in any at home activities and he'd gotten so close, with Elena's help, and now the opportunity could slip through his fingers.

He'd heard about this special summer program and this year Donovan would be old enough to attend. The program was designed for kids like him. Elena had contacts and assured him she had a way to get him in. He'd left everything to her, registration, application; he'd been too busy for the details. She was so efficient he hadn't asked any questions.

This note proved she'd kept her word. Someone in the registration department had told her to ignore the notice and said they'd put Donovan on the waiting list. They'd then provided her with a name and number to contact them and the note ended with: I know a way around this.

Elena was the key to getting him in.

"I'll do whatever is necessary for my son."

"You're right," Ava said. "She'll have you back in a heartbeat."

He blinked, surprised. He'd expected her to argue more. "You think this is a good idea?"

"Of course. Make sure Donovan's never alone with her and that she never prepares your food or drink and you should be fine," she said, her tone dripping with sarcasm. She waved. "Tell her I said 'hello.' Oh and I hope you left space on your wall for her...artwork."

The vagina abstract briefly flashed through his mind and he shivered, but then thought about Donovan's stitches from last summer.

"I don't have time. The school year's—"

"Stop saying that."

"I know it seems crazy, but it'll only be for a couple months. I'm desperate. He got rejected but this contact has him on a waiting list. With one phone call Elena can change that and make sure that he gets a slot this summer.

"I won't say anything until he gets accepted and then break up with her after it's over."

"Are you listening to yourself? Do you think you could be with someone like that?"

"Two other summer plans I'd had as backup have already fallen through. I told you I'm desperate."

"You're not getting back with Elena."

"But you got back with Folu."

She sent him a look. "You didn't hear a word I said, did you?"

"No. I'm sorry." Sort of.

She picked up the booklet and flipped through, looking at the glamorous matte pictures. "Our relationship and engagement is officially over. My family knows, my mother had a conniption, my sister got banished from the house, other than that everything is great."

He stared at her stunned. "You're not engaged?"

She waved him away. "Quiet. I have to think."

Dai watched her as she read the booklet, his mind racing. She wasn't with Folu? That's what she'd wanted to tell him? That's why she'd looked so happy?

"It does look impressive," Ava said.

Dai nodded wondering why he felt both deliriously happy and panicked at the same time. Ava was free. She wasn't getting married and she was okay with it. And she was telling him that he didn't need Elena. She was coming up with a plan, he could tell by the expression on her face. He could trust her. He wouldn't need Elena now. "It is impressive. This program began—"

Ava waved him away again. "I know, I know. I already read that part." That didn't surprise him. She was already halfway through the booklet. What would take him an hour to get through she could read and comprehend in minutes. "I'm already sold by the fact that you want Donovan in it."

She trusted his judgment that meant a lot to him. "Yeah."

She tapped her chin, thoughtful. "The founder is Alexis Taylor." She paused. "Hmm. I wonder why that name sounds familiar."

"She's the founder of the camp and—"

Ava shook her head. "No, it's something else." She snapped her fingers then grabbed her handbag and searched through it. Eventually she pulled out what she'd been searching for—a business card.

"I know her."

"How?"

"It's a long story and I only met her recently. But at least you won't have to pimp yourself. I might be able to help you after all. She owes me a favor."

25

Ava felt confident she would be able to get Alexis to make an exception for Donovan. She felt even more confident when she was able to schedule an appointment the next week and decided that she and Dai should attend the meeting together while Donovan was at school.

Her confidence fell when she picked him up that afternoon.

She stood on his front door step and stared at him. "What are you wearing?"

"What's wrong with this?"

He looked like a sexy corporate raider. She pointed to his black suit. "Everything?"

He tugged on his jacket. "I wanted to make a good impression."

"You will, but not dressed like that."

He was trying too hard but she didn't want to tell him so. "You need to change."

"We don't have enough time."

"Yes, we do. I lied to you about the time for the appointment." She pushed past him, kicked off her heels and headed up the stairs barefoot.

She walked into his bedroom.

"You lied to me?" Dai asked, following her into the room.

"It was for your own good." She shuffled through his closet. "Where's your peach short sleeve shirt?"

"In the hamper."

"The green?"

"Same."

"The turquoise linen?"

"Dry cleaners. Wait, have you memorized the clothes in my wardrobe?"

Almost. "No, I just know the effect I'm going for. I want you to look like a father."

"I am a father."

"Right now you look like the godfather of a criminal enterprise."

"Thank you."

"It's not a compliment."

"I'll still take it as one."

She grabbed a more casual dress shirt. "Here, put this on."

He peeled off his jacket. "Okay. Where are you going?" he asked when she turned to leave. "You can stay."

"I'll meet you downstairs."

He followed her into the hall.

He grinned, unbuttoning his shirt. "Feeling shy all of a sudden? You've seen me shirtless before."

"It's not the same."

"What makes it different?"

"Stop playing and get changed."

He laughed. "Thanks for this," he said before he kissed her and she let him. Their lips touched for a brief, tender moment filled with the intimacy and affection of a long married couple.

Dai spun around and walked a few steps then halted, as if finally realizing what he'd just done. What he'd never done before.

Ava held her breath. *Don't turn around. Don't turn around.* If he didn't turn around then they could both pretend that it hadn't happened. That it hadn't felt so natural. So sweet, so wonderful. She swallowed, willing him to take another step forward. *Go back into your room.*

But he didn't.

Dai slowly turned around. He walked up to her, his eyes revealing everything she felt, his deep voice filled with longing. "Can I do that again?"

Yes, please. Wait. No. No that would be wrong. It would change everything. Ava tried not to glimpse at the beautiful column of brown skin peeking out from the gap of his unbuttoned shirt. She pulled the two sides together, as if closing a curtain on something forbidden. "No," she said, but her fingers wouldn't release him. She looked at his lips, then his chest then his lips again. Her words sounding breathless when she said, "We can't. It wouldn't be right."

"You really think that?"

She nodded. "You should go."

"Then you have to let me go."

"It didn't happen," she said, still holding onto his shirt, not meeting his eyes.

Dai sighed. He wouldn't misunderstand her wish. She wanted to erase the kiss from memory. "Okay."

"It can't happen."

"Okay."

Ava lifted her gaze. Met his eyes. "You mean too much to me."

"You mean a lot to me too."

"So we have to protect what we have. One wrong move and

—" She loosened her fingers, releasing her grip, and smoothed down the wrinkles on his shirt. "Go and get changed."

"You think pretending will make it go away?"

She cupped his cheek. "There's no pretending because nothing happened. Remember?"

He bit his lip and nodded. "I hope you're right."

She smiled, her voice light and cheerful. "Nothing happened so nothing's changed."

Dai stared at her for a long moment and Ava held her breath fearing he'd kiss her again and this time it wouldn't be quick and she wouldn't stop him.

She was the first to look away. She rested her hands on his shoulders and spun him around. "Go on. Don't take long."

To her relief he walked inside the bedroom and closed the door. She released a breath. A minefield diverted.

She could forget this.

Unfortunately, her lips remembered.

Dai resisted the urge to bang his head against the wall. What the hell had come over him?

Nothing's changed. That's what she'd told him. But of course that was wrong. Things had already changed. Even before the kiss.

The kiss wasn't really saying 'Thank you,' but rather 'I love you.' They both knew that but Ava didn't want to face it and Dai wasn't ready to admit it.

Instead it hadn't happened.

Dai bit his fist and silently swore. What was he going to do? Instead of getting better, things were getting worse. It was one thing to be attracted to your best friend. It was something else to fall in love with her.

But he'd been fooling himself.

He'd been in love with her for a long time.

When she'd told him about her broken engagement he'd been surprised by how relieved he'd felt. He'd thought it was because he'd never really taken to Folu but he now realized it was more than that. He didn't want anyone else to have her. He'd liked Elena, convinced himself he loved her, because he was ready to settle down again, but after their breakup he'd hardly missed her. What was wrong with him?

"Are you having trouble with your buttons?" Ava asked through the door as if she were a teacher and he a kindergartner.

He laughed; relieved she could still tease him. "I'm getting there."

"Well, hurry up or I'm coming in."

Dai hastily buttoned up the shirt she'd given him then opened the door. "See?"

Ava looked him up and down. "You call this a good impression?"

"You're the one who chose the shirt."

"And you buttoned it wrong."

She began to unbutton it.

"The other shirt was better."

"For a crime lord." She patted his chest. "That's better."

"You know treating me like a kid doesn't make me any less of a man."

Ava affectionately patted him on the cheek. "Sure it does."

Dai couldn't resist a laugh, feeling some tension ease.

What they had was too special. And she wasn't ready. He wouldn't risk losing her.

He would get over this.

26

———

"You have to get out of the car."

Dai didn't move, his hands still gripping the steering wheel. He had parked the car under a tree, the unassuming building that held the Boulders and Bridges headquarters only a few yards away. "We still have time. You said we were early."

Ava sighed exasperated. "That was nearly twenty minutes ago."

He took a deep breath but it didn't help. He still couldn't move. He needed this interview to work.

Ava opened the passenger side. "Let's go."

"About the kiss."

She stared at him blank. "What kiss?"

He frowned. "Don't pretend it didn't happen."

"We agreed nothing happened."

Dai shook his head. "I changed my mind. I can't stop thinking about it."

"You're using it as a distraction because you're nervous." Ava stepped out and closed the door then opened the driver's side. "We're not talking about that right now. Stop stalling.

Come on." She tugged on his arm. "I know how much you hate interviews."

Dai reluctantly got out of the car and closed the door. He didn't just hate interviews. He loathed them. As well as parent-teacher meetings, doctor visits, and therapy sessions (the ones he'd taken with his ex-wife had been particularly awful).

Anything where he had to sit in front of someone and talk and possibly try to impress them. He usually made a terrible first impression, which was why he ended up working for himself. But he couldn't handle everything on his own.

"What if I make her cry?" he said, following Ava as she marched towards the building.

"You're not going to make her cry."

"It's happened before."

"It's not going to happen this time."

"What if I scare her?"

"As long as you let me do the talking you'll be fine. Just remember not to lean forward."

"Lean forward?"

"Yes, you do that when you're really interested in something but sometimes it can appear aggressive. Try to relax."

"That's not going to happen." He halted. "I probably shouldn't have come. Perhaps if you—"

Ava grabbed his hand before he could turn back to the car. "You said you'd do anything for Donovan."

Dai took a deep breath.

"You can do this."

He squeezed her hand. She was his anchor and his greatest support. She believed in him. He suddenly felt unstoppable. He took a step forward. "Let's go."

~

HE HADN'T LET GO.

He still held her hand.

Ava wasn't sure if Dai'd forgotten or not, but felt no need to pull away when they sat down in the waiting area outside Alexis' office.

Dai stared straight ahead. But his gaze was the only part of him that managed to stay still. He leaned back, then forward, rubbed his forehead, his chin, tapped his foot, chewed his lip. But he stared at the wall and didn't release her hand.

Strangely she didn't mind. He wasn't talking, which was good that meant he was thinking about his son, which was even better. It meant that by the end of the day, the kiss would be forgotten.

Sort of.

Ava closed her eyes, silently praying that calling Alexis had been a good idea. But her mind wouldn't focus on Alexis. Instead it remembered the pressure of his lips. The kiss had been brief but so sweet. She wondered how it would feel to have his warm body wrapped around her...

"Thinking about the kiss?" Dai whispered, his breath warm against her ear.

Ava's eyes flew open, heat burning her cheeks. "What? No," she said, playfully punching him and making him laugh.

HIS TEASING eyes made it clear he didn't believe her. She didn't care, basking in the glow of his gaze. His eyes brightened (she loved when his eyes smiled at her like that) glad he didn't look worried.

She pulled her hand away and folded her arms.

He feigned a look of hurt. "Aw, is that my punishment for teasing you?"

"You don't need to hold my hand."

"But I like holding it." He held out his hand. "Please."

Before she could respond, Alexis came out of her office.

The woman that finally greeted them looked like a completely different person. Nothing like the depressed woman at the hospital. Her hair fell to her shoulders in a layered cut; her face looked arresting and refined.

"It's so wonderful to see you again!" she greeted warmly. She hugged Ava then ushered her inside the comfortable and inviting office.

"You too. How is your father?"

"Much better thank you."

Alexis turned to Dai. "Ava spoke highly about you. But she didn't mention your son." She glanced at Ava. "Your fiancé is a two for one deal I see."

Dai blinked. "Um...no she's not—"

"I didn't want to appear as if I was trying to get special favors," Ava quickly said.

"That's commendable. You wouldn't believe the kind of bribes I get from desperate parents. Please take a seat."

They did.

"I like to have these little discussions so that parents can get a broader picture of our vision here. It's more indepth than what you can see in a brochure or find online."

Dai clasped his hands and leaned forward with the cool intent of a serpent ready to strike. "Is that right?"

Ava saw the woman's eye widen in uncertainty. Her words faltered. "Uh...yes. And—" Her cell phone rang. "Oh, could you excuse me a moment?"

"Sure."

Ava took the moment to lightly rest a hand on his thigh before she squeezed hard. He jerked and glanced at her. She motioned to the back of the chair and mouthed "Lean back."

He sighed and did.

Alexis rested her cell phone down. "Sorry about that."

"Please go on," Ava said.

Alexis began to share more about the program and Ava could sense Dai getting restless.

He shifted in his seat then rubbed his hands on his thighs, which always made him look bored and impatient. Ava grabbed his hand and as she knew it would, the action calmed him.

But she knew it wouldn't last long. Before Alexis could get her second wind, Ava said, "We're sold," interrupting her. "We love everything about the program. Did you get the video we sent?"

"Yes, Donovan seems wonderful. I'd be pleased to accept your little boy for next summer."

Dai jerked forward as if propelled by a rocket. "Next summer?!"

Alexis jumped, startled.

"We need it for this summer," Ava explained gently, "I apologize for not being more forthcoming on the phone."

Alexis frowned. "I'm afraid it's too late. We're fully—"

"But we were on a waiting list," Dai said. "I thought there might be a cancellation or—"

She frowned. "You were on our waiting list?"

"Yes."

"Give me a minute." She turned to her computer screen. "Yes...here it is. The waiting list. Umm. I don't see your son's name here. No wait a minute. It was and then it was removed by parent's request. An E. Cardoza?"

Dai turned green. Elena had gotten her revenge.

Ava patted his hand. "Honey, could you give us a minute?"

He stared at her, looking devastated and unsure.

She smiled in reassurance.

He stood and turned to Alexis. "It doesn't even have to be

for the entire term. He'll be with his mother for a week. I will pay whatever—"

"Honey," Ava said with more force. She didn't want him to appear desperate although she knew he was. She stood and pretended to be kissing him on the cheek, while instead whispering, "Trust me."

His eyes met and held hers. For a moment she thought he would kiss her again, as an intense, heated look of trust burned through any lingering worry and fear.

The darkness of his gaze would have frightened someone else, but to her the expression in his eyes was as intimate as if he'd cupped her face and made a vow with the ferocity of a warrior headed to battle that said, I'll never doubt you.

He left her shaken and longing to be the person he thought she was. Folu didn't like her strength. Dai depended on it. She would not fail him.

He squeezed her arm, a gentle reassuring act that made her body grow hot, before he turned and left.

The moment the door closed Ava returned to her seat and said, "I'll be honest. We're desperate. But I understand you're in a bind. I will volunteer my services in exchange for letting Donovan come for even half days here. He's really excited about attending camp. It's all he's been talking about and I'll do whatever it takes."

Alexis tapped a finger against the desk. "I'm listening."

"I work with kids and teens as a psychotherapist." And with her reduced clientele she had the time. "I can send you my credentials. I have passed stringent background checks. Not to boast but I'm good at what I do."

Alexis grinned. "Does Dai know how lucky he is to have you?"

"Most times. When he forgets I remind him."

She looked thoughtful. "Well, we do have a separate list

and offer special privileges to those who work for us. There are two students who've aged out of the program and Donovan will soon be your son anyway so I think I can make this work."

"Thank you."

"Of course I'll want a wedding invite."

Ava laughed nervously. "Right. It's still a ways off."

"I'm kidding. We could use the help. A lot of our kids are dealing with more tension and anxiety than usual. We'll have to sort out the schedule and it might be trying at times."

"I'm used to that."

Alexis held out her hand. "Okay, then welcome aboard."

27

———

Ava found Dai prowling the length of the grounds like a caged lion. He halted when he saw her. He didn't speak. Fear. Hope. Scattering over his face. Their eyes met across the distance.

He slowly walked towards her.

She decided to take him out of his misery. She gave him the "Okay" sign.

He broke into a run.

She glanced around hoping they were alone then waved her hands for him to stop.

He kept running.

Her heart pounded as the distance between them swiftly disappeared.

He didn't stop running until he was close enough to grab her and spin her around.

"Calm down," Ava said, hugging him back and laughing.

Dai held her tighter. "You don't know how much this means to both of us," he said, his breath warm against her cheek.

"I do. Now put me down."

He sighed. "Do I have to?"

"Yes."

When her feet touched the ground again she felt a little dizzy and knew it wasn't only from being spun around. She felt strangely giddy, remembering the touch of his lips from this afternoon, the feel of his arms. She'd never been aware of him like this before. She knew he could be as exuberant as his son, but she'd always taken it in stride.

But this time felt different. Was it a sense of relief? Glad that she'd managed to help him? Or something infinitely more dangerous?

She felt like she'd gone into battle and come back and he was proud of her. He didn't find her too strong. He trusted her. Depended on her. It was an intoxicating feeling. So few people treated her that way.

"How did you do it?" Dai said.

Ava hesitated. That was the one tiny snag in her plan: The lie. "I'll tell you in the car."

IT WAS like watching a scene from a movie.

Alexis clasped her hands behind her back as she stared out the window. She'd never seen two people so much in love. She'd worried about her rash actions.

There were few things Alexis trusted, but seeing Ava and Dai together she knew accepting their son had been one of the best decisions she'd made in a long time.

28

———

Ava never looked more beautiful to him than she did at that moment but Dai had a sneaking suspicion she was avoiding his gaze.

They hadn't made it back to the car. Instead she'd suggested they take a walk. There was plenty to see, the building giving way to a lush expanse of green, stately trees and a large pond reflecting the rays of the sun.

But Ava didn't look at any of it. She kept her head bent.

"What's wrong?" he finally asked her.

She bit her lip. "I lied."

Dai felt his legs grow weak, his head started to spin. "You mean Donovan didn't get in?"

She looped her arm through his. "No, no," she said quickly. "I'd never lie about that."

He took a deep breath, feeling the world return to normal. "What is it then?"

"About her thinking you're my fiancée—"

He sighed. "Yes, about that."

"It was the only way I could get her to agree to let Donovan in."

"And that bothers you?"

"No, it's just..."

"It's okay," he said quickly, not wanting to lose this chance. "No one needs to know that we lied. It's not like we have a bunch of parent-kid events to attend. We don't have to appear as a couple since Donovan will be picked up by the bus and...Why are you frowning like that?"

"I also volunteered my services so I'll be working here possibly once a week. We have to make sure to keep this lie from him. However, Alexis doesn't run the camp and the likelihood of her saying anything to him is slim. I think it's safe to keep this between us. I don't want him to have to lie. We have to be very careful so—" She looked at him when he abruptly stopped. "What?"

"You'll be working here?"

"As a volunteer. I had to sweeten the pot."

"How many hours?"

"Don't know yet."

He shook his head. "No, you're busy as it is as a psychologist."

"I'm a psychotherapist."

"Are you sure she won't take a donation? Money's not a problem." He began to turn.

Ava grabbed his arm. "It's okay. It's better this way. I don't mind."

He swore. "But that's not what—"

She squeezed his arm. "It's worth it and my schedule is flexible." She didn't want him to know she had the time. She brought in enough money from high powered clients that the clinic where she worked didn't care about her reduced hours.

She looked around the expansive grounds. "I can see Donovan having a great time here."

"But you'll have to pretend all summer."

"It's okay. I'll survive eight weeks."

"Like I said, he'll spend a week with his mother in August. But if she finds out we lied before then..."

"She won't." Ava playfully poked him in the side. " But I'll be crimping your style. If you meet a sexy single mother—"

"Stop right there. After Elena I'm taking myself off the market for a while. Dating is the last thing on my mind."

"I guess you could use a break. We both could."

He kissed her on the lips. Lightly, tenderly.

Ava looked at him surprised. "What's that for?"

Dai's eyes danced with mischief. "Just thanking my *fiancée* the best way I know how."

Donovan's scream of delight could have pierced Ava's eardrums but his joy had been worth the pain. They'd decided to tell him the moment he returned home from school.

He jumped, he spun in circles, and he made up a crazy dance.

"There's a lake," he said.

He'd told her that many times but Ava still smiled and said, "Yes, I know."

"And there are going to be lots of trails and things to do."

"Yes."

"And there's a lake."

"Your dad worked really hard to get you in so do your best not to get into trouble."

He was playing air guitar and not listening. Ava hadn't

really expected him to. It usually took him a while to calm down after excitement like this.

Dai smiled at her. "You made a little boy's dream come true."

And their plan would have worked perfectly if Mrs. Dayo hadn't gotten a root canal.

29

———————

IT WAS TOO beautiful a day for a disaster, a cool breeze tempering the heat of the summer sun, but disaster struck anyway.

Because of Mrs. Dayo's root canal Ava found herself helping her mother run errands for her. It was usually a task given to Cat, but because of Ava's broken engagement, her mother had assigned Ava to come with her almost as punishment as if to say: This will be your fate if you don't find another man soon.

And Ava, in no mood to argue, let her. She'd already managed to attend a housewarming party (where she'd spotted Maya and Keeden being chummier than she'd ever thought they could be) and a baby shower without much drama and her reputation intact. Most people felt sorry for her rather than thinking she was in anyway the cause for being newly single again.

She and her mother had picked up Mrs. Dayo's dry cleaning, bought items for her garden and had finished grocery shopping for items for a special stew her mother wanted to make.

Ava was helping her mother load the trunk, making the car sink under the weight of the many bags, when she heard someone say her name.

She turned and saw Alexis. Suddenly she felt no breeze and the sun felt as if it could burn off her skin.

She wanted to jump into the trunk and close the hood.

"Ava," Alexis said, coming closer. "I thought it was you." She hugged her as if they were old friends.

"Yes, well I don't want to keep you."

Her mother stepped forward, making it clear she expected an introduction.

"Th-this is my mother," Ava said. "Mom this is Alexis Taylor."

Alexis smiled at her. "A pleasure. You must be so proud of your daughter."

Her mother nodded. "I am. Most times."

"You're being modest. The way she helps others is a credit to you." She looked at Ava. "How is Donovan enjoying things?"

Over the last three weeks he couldn't stop talking. Especially about his new best friend. "He's been over the moon."

"I'm glad. And you've been a great help as well. The kids really enjoy talking to you. I'm glad your fiancé is willing to share you with us." She winked. "It was a pleasure meeting him."

"Yes, yes," Ava said quickly, sending her mother a nervous glance.

Alexis' cell phone rang. She checked the number then said, "Ugh, it's my sister adding more to an already long list of things I have to pick up for Dad. Talk again soon." She headed to the store's entrance.

Her mother slowly turned to her. She clasped her hands together and raised her eyes to the sky. "I knew you wouldn't disappoint me." She hopped around in a circle before raising her hands to the sky.

"Mom, stop it," Ava said looking around the parking lot.

"Praise God. My prayers have been answered. You will not be a shame to me. I knew I needn't have worried that that sister of yours had tainted your mind. Why didn't you tell me?"

"It's not what you think."

"How can it not be? She said she met your fiancé when you'd only told us weeks ago you'd broken up." Her mother pulled out her cell phone. "I must call—"

"No, please don't."

"Why not?"

"Because it's not him."

"It's not who?"

"Folu."

She frowned. "What do you mean it's not Folu? You have another fiancé?"

Ava hesitated. "In a manner of speaking."

"What? Stop speaking in riddles."

"It's no one. I'd really prefer not to talk about it yet."

"A secret? When have you started keeping secrets from your mother?"

You wouldn't believe me if I told you. "It's complicated."

"Is he married?" She pointed at her. "You have no business with a married man. If they can break one vow they can break another. And they will always tell you they will marry you someday. Don't believe them they just want—"

"I'm not seeing a married man."

Her mother started to smile. "I know. You made him up to save face, didn't you?"

"Right. Something like that."

She frowned. "But then that white woman said she'd met him. How could she have met him before me?"

"You'll meet him if it works out. I didn't want to let anyone else know because it was so sudden after my breakup with Folu."

"Well, at least you're taking marriage seriously, unlike your sister. I am relieved to hear it and as long as it's not that bald man with the ridiculous son I will have no qualms." She'd heard Alexis mention Donovan but thankfully made no connection since he didn't register as important.

Ava couldn't believe her mother could reduce an attractive, successful single father like Dai to "that bald man with the crazy son." She felt her temper rise but kept it under control. Dai might be bald but it didn't take away from his appeal, at least not in her eyes and Donovan was a high spirited kid with lots of clever ideas. But she couldn't stand up for the father, without her mother getting suspicious; however, she could stand up for the son.

"Donovan isn't ridiculous. He's very bright."

"He could exhaust a swarm of bees. He can't sit still. Hardly stops talking. Remember when he broke a tea cup?"

"He glued it back together."

"It doesn't matter. We're talking about your new fiancé not that bald friend of yours."

"Stop calling him bald."

"He is bald, isn't he?"

"He's also gorgeous, funny and smart."

Her mother sniffed.

And she was reminded of how her family thought of people without advanced degrees. "He is smart," Ava repeated. "He owns a very lucrative business and has made a great life for himself. You shouldn't reduce him to one characteristic. I thought you liked Dai."

"I do. He's a hard worker, but you're not so desperate to have to settle for a man which such baggage."

She thought of telling her mother the truth: "I was helping Dai get Donovan into a special summer camp and sort of posed as a couple to do it," then realized her mother wasn't the most understanding of people and didn't want her to know Dai's business.

Her mother clapped her hands together. "I forgot the bell peppers!"

"I think we have some at home."

"Green ones. I need yellow and orange." She hurried back towards the store before Ava could stop her.

As Ava hurried after her she saw a familiar figure also enter the sliding glass doors.

Dai.

That's when she started to run.

30

———

Alexis and her mother could not see Dai at the same time.

Ava frantically searched the aisles and eventually found him in the condiments section. She grabbed his arm. "What are you doing here?"

He stared at her shocked. "Shopping. It's sort of customary in places like this."

"You rarely shop here."

"I'm picking up something for Auntie," he said. "And I don't have a lot of time. I left Donovan with her. He's good with her and likes playing with her dog, but I have about thirty-five minutes before I start to worry that he'll get into trouble."

That made sense. He still checked on the mother of his former boss, the mechanic who'd allowed him to work in his car shop when he was in high school. His former boss, who'd been like a father to him as well as a friend, had suffered a stroke several years back, and had asked Dai to check on his mother from time to time and they'd soon become friends and he treated her like a grandmother.

Ava pushed him in the direction of the exit. "Go, I'll buy it for you."

"It's more than one thing." He narrowed his eyes. "What's gotten into you?"

Ava heard someone gasp and turned and saw Alexis. "There you are! We were just talking about you," she said.

Dai frowned. "You were?"

"Yes, Ava introduced me to her mother."

His voice cracked and his brows shot up. "You met her *mother?*"

Alexis took a step back, startled by his outburst. Ava grabbed his hand and patted his cheek. "Yes, darling but it's okay."

"Really?"

"Yes." Ava kept her voice light and turned to Alexis. "You know how in-laws can be. She frightens him a little."

Alexis grinned. "I met her and she frightens me a lot."

Ava laughed and tried to take the hand basket from him. "So let me finish your shopping."

"Seeing you two together," Alexis said, "I think you should just elope. Don't let your family get in the way."

Spoken like a true American romantic with their proud individualism and "love conquers all" belief. Ava knew it wasn't that simple but appreciated the sentiment.

Ava was about to reply when she saw her mother walk past the aisle searching for her. Before her mother could do a double take Ava spun Dai around and kissed him so that his back was to her mother and his body would hide her.

The kiss was just for show. It barely lasted seconds. Certainly not enough time to register how sweet his lips tasted, the scent of his skin, the warmth of his body. But she took it all in and more. When his arm snaked around her waist, she came back to her senses.

She peeked over his shoulder when she was certain her mother was safely away then stepped back and said,

"Did you hear that, darling? We don't have to have a big wedding."

His dark gaze held her still. He made the kiss feel real, the heat in his gaze briefly made her forget they weren't alone, that kissing him hadn't been part of a performance. Out of the corner of her eye she saw a row of red bottles of hot sauce each seeming to describe how she felt—Red hot, Calypso hot, Smokin' jalapeno hot.

She couldn't tear her eyes away even when he cupped her cheek and said in a deep, velvet voice, "If you want to elope just say the word."

Her heart beat wildly. This wasn't Dai. This was somebody else. Somebody with ink black lashes and brows who made her want to forget pretending to be sweet and good all the time. This man was a dangerous temptation.

Clean up on aisle three.

The voiceover announcement returned her to her senses again.

Ava forced a nervous laugh and turned to Alexis. "He likes to pretend he doesn't want a big wedding even though he loves a great party." She held up her hand before either of them could speak. "Excuse me for a minute," she said then hurried down the aisle to find her mother.

She found her in the bakery department surrounded by the scent of fresh donuts and rolls.

Her mother saw her and scowled. "Where did you disappear to? Why are you breathing like that? It's very unbecoming."

Ava took a deep breath. "Met an old friend." She paused and took another breath. "I didn't want to lose them."

"Which old friend?"

Ava looked into her mother's basket. "Have you found everything you need?"

"Yes, but—"

"Good, go home without me."

"No, I'll wait in the car."

"It's too hot."

"Let me meet this old friend of yours."

"Really not necessary, Mom." Ava pulled out her cell phone and started to type, telling her mother what she was texting. "Just wanted you to know Mom's coming home with a lot of bags and she'll need your help with them. Be ready. Thanks." She put her phone away. "There. Cat will be expecting you so I'll see you later."

"Don't think I've forgotten about your fiancé."

"I'll explain more when I get home."

To her relief her mother headed to the self-checkout without arguing.

Ava returned to Dai and Alexis, breathless. She held up a toothpaste box. "It's on sale and there was only one left," she lied.

"Dental hygiene is important to her," Dai said sending Ava a curious look.

"Yes."

"We don't want to keep you." She grabbed Dai's arm. "Great seeing you." She spun around and hurried down the aisle, pulling him along with her.

"Should I even ask?" Dai said.

"Not yet. We still have enough time left to finish what's on your list."

She helped him select a few more items then they both headed to the check-out.

Ava halted when she spotted her mother. Ahh! What was she still doing here?

She'd clearly added things to her basket and now was having trouble at the self-check out. Her mother always had trouble with the chip reader.

Ava shoved Dai to the side, hiding him behind one of the large summer barbecue displays before her mother could see him and said to him, "I need some lotion and mouthwash. Could you get them for me?"

Dai checked his watch. "I'm not sure—"

"We still have enough time. I promise."

"Okay, where are you going?"

"Just checking on something, I'll be right there." She gently shoved him again. "Go on."

Dai shook his head then left.

Ava dashed forward, helped her mother finish buying her purchases then helped her to her car. She didn't breathe until she saw her mother drive away then she returned to the store and saw Dai helping an older woman get almond flour from a high shelf.

She noticed the woman admiring his physique. The woman asked him to get two more items but when the woman 'accidentally' dropped her pen then watched Dai bend over and pick it up, like he was a slice of cheesecake and she was a woman with a sweet tooth, Ava decided to end the show.

"Come on, honey," she said. "Let's go."

She saw the other woman's face fall in disappointment.

"I was just helping this lady with a few things," he said, referring to the attractive woman in a green summer dress and sandals. "Are you okay now?"

"Yes," the woman said amused by his innocence, then gripped the handles of her cart and sauntered down the aisle.

"Oh dear," Ava said. "I think I just ruined her day."

"What about mine?"

She spun to him. "What?"

Dai didn't look angry, but the captivated heated gaze hadn't left. If she wasn't careful she could kiss him again and she wouldn't be pretending.

His gaze dipped to her lips then returned back to her eyes. "Are you ready to tell me what's going on?"

She couldn't look at him and wasn't ready to talk about her rash action yet. She pretended to look at the time. "Time's running out. You'd better buy these items. I'll tell you on the way to Auntie's."

He grabbed her wrist before she could leave. "No, *darling*. You're going to tell me now."

She took his basket to give herself something to do. It was easier than looking at him. "There's a problem. My mother found out that I have a new fiancé." She glanced at him before she shifted her gaze to a row of cooking sprays. "I didn't tell her it's you though, but I'm going to have to come up with something soon. I thought of telling her the truth but my mother isn't the best with secrets and I don't want to jeopardize Donovan's situation."

Dai took the basket from her. "I see." He headed down the aisle.

She followed him. It was easier talking to his back. "I kissed you because I didn't want her to see us."

"Hmm."

"I'm sorry I startled you."

Dai stopped and sent her a hooded glance. "Is that what you think happened just now?"

Ava blinked. "I don't know what you mean."

He flashed a slow, grin. "Alright Ava. Let's go back to pretending." He turned and continued down the aisle before he added in a low voice. "For now."

31

To Dai's relief Auntie's split level grey house still looked in order, outside he'd heard Donovan playing with her little dog, Felix, in the back garden, the dog happily yipping in response.

Inside they were greeted by the smell of spicy peanut cookies and the sound of a television drama on the TV: A melodrama from the sound of the crying and wailing.

"We're back," Dai said, walking past the living room as they headed to the kitchen with the grocery bags.

The older woman in the armchair beamed over at him and proudly said, "Anyeongasayo," waving hello.

Ava smiled while Dai shook his head and called back, "Still not Korean, Auntie."

It had been a running joke. She was an ardent watcher of South Korean dramas since the eighties and was determined to speak to him in her bits and pieces of Korean even though he was half-Japanese-American.

Ava set a bag on the counter. "That joke is old enough to be buried in a pyramid."

Dai shrugged. "I don't mind."

Ava lowered her voice. "You should confuse her for a Ghanaian or worse yet Igbo."

Dai opened the fridge and began putting items away. "Really doesn't bother me." He closed the door then looked out the window and saw poor Felix, a small, shaggy brown mutt, growing tired. He opened the sliding glass door. "Come on and give Felix some water."

Donovan came bounding into the kitchen, then paused when he saw Ava.

"Sandy! I didn't know you were here."

"I just came."

"Guess what I—"

"You can tell me while you're giving Felix some water," Ava gently interrupted him.

"Oh right." He refilled Felix's water bowl, spilling half of it while also telling her how he'd helped Auntie catch a cockroach in the basement when they went down there to get extra sugar. She stocked a lot of her bulk purchases in the basement, and kept enough extra items to feed a neighborhood.

"It was a little scary but I didn't mind."

"Good job," Ava said, handing him a rag to mop up the extra water, while the little dog raced forward and lapped it up as if it had crossed the Kalahari Desert. "She likes having you."

Donovan straightened, puffing his chest out. "Because I'm smart and I play with Felix and I help her out. She needs me."

"Yes." Ava took the rag from him and handed him a glass of fruit punch. "Think you can drink this without spilling it?"

He looked offended. "Of course I can," he said then promptly dribbled some juice down the front of his shirt, leaving a bright pink stain on his white and grey T-shirt.

Dai sighed. "Give it to me." He shook his head. "Don't argue."

Donovan reluctantly handed back the glass. Dai gave him a juice pouch instead. "Now go and sit with Auntie."

"Can I play my game?"

"Yes, after you finish drinking."

"Alright." He raced out of the room.

"Sorry about that," Ava said. "I filled the glass too much."

"No, you didn't. My son is a klutz."

"Shh. He could hear you."

"Not a chance. The moment he starts moving he's long gone."

Ava laughed. "You're right. I remember when he started walking, he moved so fast, I could have sworn he had wheels instead of feet."

"That's why his mother tied him up."

Ava began to laugh again before she realized he wasn't joking. "At least he doesn't remember."

"Too bad I do."

Dai had called her up furious when he'd discovered what his ex-wife had been doing. It had taken Ava nearly an hour to calm him down. "She was doing her best. She didn't hurt him. He thought it was a game."

Dai rubbed his nose. "What are you going to do about our engagement?"

"It's been working out well so far, I'll have to stall my mother for a few more weeks."

"You think that's even possible?"

"I can try." Ava cupped his face. "We've come this far. Donovan's happy. You're happy."

Dai wrapped a hand around her wrist. "You think I'm happy?"

She steeled herself from the searing heat of his palm and searched his gaze, confused, even though she wanted to look away. Her pulse quickening. "Aren't you?"

He briefly shut his eyes as if pained. "I should be but..." He stared at her. "You look tired. Your mother is wearing you out, isn't she?"

Ava pulled herself free, rubbing her wrist, trying to wrest control of her heart again. "I can handle her."

"Plus, I've barely been able to reach you in weeks. You won't respond to my calls or texts because you're too busy at work and at the camp."

She plastered on a smile. "It's for a good cause."

"Then how come I get the feeling you're avoiding me?"

She stepped back. "That's not what I'm doing. You worry too much."

Dai pointed to her. "Then why are you moving away from me?"

Ava took another step back before she stopped and folded her arms. "I'm not, I'm just—" She tugged on her shirt. "I'm sweating from running back and forth in the shop."

He held her gaze and lowered his voice. "It's me, Ava. Don't lie to me. Something's changed."

She rested her hands on her hips. "No, it hasn't." But it had since that day when they first met Alexis. When he was near it never felt near enough. She'd become more aware of him—from the sound of his voice, the shape of his hands, the way he moved, and definitely the way he said her name. It shouldn't make her skin tingle; it shouldn't make her think of muscular thighs wrapped around her and the smooth sensation of bed sheets sliding off her back.

Dai shook his head, frustrated. "I've never heard of a fake relationship were the couple stay away from each other."

"That's not what's happening here. We both agreed I should keep my distance until the end of summer."

"You didn't have to kiss me."

"It was the first thing I could think of," she said annoyed

with herself and him. "We're engaged after all, right? I wanted it to look real and hide from my mother. It won't happen again."

He took a step forward, his gaze dropping to her lips. "And if I want it to?"

"You don't. I'm not going to be your woman on the rebound."

His eyes flashed. "That's what you think of me? I'm on the prowl for some—"

"No," Ava said quickly. "I know you wouldn't need me for that." She released a nervous laugh. "Have you called that woman you met at Koji's party?"

Dai leaned against the counter and slowly blinked.

"I guess that's a no."

He continued to stare at her, making her anxiety increase. She didn't like when he got angry. "I'm sorry. I didn't mean it like that. I liked it too but it was just stress relief."

His gaze and voice fell flat. "Stress relief?"

"Yes. Now go. It's too quiet." She gently nudged him towards the door. "You should check on Auntie and Donovan, I'll be right there."

He didn't move. Instead he crossed one ankle over the other and continued to study her.

Ava licked her lip, feeling the weight of his gaze. "Dai."

"What?"

"Please." *Please don't make this any harder than it needs to be. Please let's keep pretending that nothing's changed. Please don't make me face what I'm not ready to.*

To her relief, he pushed himself from the counter and left without a word.

32

———

He wouldn't push her. She wasn't ready. But what if she was never ready? Could he pretend that his feelings for her hadn't changed? He wasn't like her. He wasn't good at burying his emotions. Hiding how he really felt.

But he couldn't be reckless. He didn't want to lose her. And if that meant pretending a little longer than he wanted to, he would.

Dai marched into the living room where Felix napped under a painting of a musician playing a talking drum, Auntie watched her drama, and Donovan wore headphones and played on his game set.

"We put everything away," he said.

"Eolmayeyo?" she asked.

Dai bent and kissed the hefty woman with four thick grey braids and a sweet smile, on the cheek before taking a seat. "Still not Korean, Auntie. But you don't have to worry about the price. You know I've got you covered."

"Are you well?" she said, switching to English. "You look underfed."

"I'm fine."

"And your mother?"

"Also well, thank you."

"Dynamite is a joy," she said, calling Donovan by the wrong nickname as usual.

Ava came into the room carrying a tray of drinks. She set the tray down on the coffee table next to the bowl of snacks Dai had put out before he'd left to go grocery shopping. She handed the older woman a glass of iced ginger tea. "His nickname is Dynamo, Auntie." Ava handed Dai a glass before grabbing her own and sitting down next to him on the retro styled beige sofa.

"Dynamo?" She frowned. "I never understood that word."

"Actually, it's very simple," Dai said. "It's an electrical generator that creates—"

Ava playfully slapped Dai on the chest, halting his explanation, which she knew would be anything but simple, and said, "It just means a very energetic person."

"Right," Dai agreed.

Auntie nodded and said, "So when are you two getting married?"

Dai choked on his drink while Ava froze with her glass halfway to her mouth.

They both sent a panicked glance at Donovan, but he remained oblivious as he continued playing his game.

Then their eyes met with a shared look of *What do we do now?* Ava's gaze sharpened and her eyes silently said, *Relax, Dai, it's going to be okay.* Dai's eyes widened and said, *How will it be okay?!!* Ava held her gaze steady and continued with, *Mom couldn't have told anyone yet* as Dai's brown gaze darkened with doubt saying *Are you sure?* Ava blinked. *Of course I'm sure.* Dai frowned, narrowing his eyes. *Then why would she say that?* But Ava remained unconcerned and replied with a pointed look, *Trust me. I never told her who I was engaged to,* before she took a deep breath and turned to Auntie and said aloud, "You heard about the engagement?"

Auntie clapped her hands delighted. "So you *are* engaged finally?"

"No, wait. What?"

"You said you were engaged."

"But *you* asked when are we getting married," Ava said.

She nodded. "Yes, it's about time now that you're both free."

"Auntie, you've watched too many dramas. That's not going to happen."

"But you are engaged." She grinned like a naughty child. "I overheard you in the kitchen."

"Oh, that...um..." Ava lowered her voice. "The truth is I had to pose as his fiancé to get Donovan into a special summer program but after it's over the charade will end." She glanced at Donovan. "He doesn't know that and neither does anyone else. Promise not to tell anyone?"

She nodded. "Your mother may have to get used to him being part Korean."

Dai took a long swallow of his tea then set it down. "Not Korean, Auntie."

"It's not real," Ava said. "So it won't be a problem at all. We just have a few more weeks to go."

"Shame you have to hide your love," Auntie said, patting her chest as if heartbroken.

Ava shook her head at the stubborn woman. "We're not hiding anything."

"It's like this drama I just watched," she said, ignoring her, and then told them the plot.

Ava sighed. "Why can't you watch Bollywood movies like a normal Nigerian your age?"

"I watch those too and the Nollywood ones as well. And there was this story—"

Ava shook her head sorry she'd said anything. "I'll get us some more sweet biscuits."

She left.

Dai watched the emotive funeral scene on the television surprised by how familiar it felt. He'd never watched the series before but the cadence of the words and feelings felt like something he'd heard before.

Then he realized why. He *had* heard it before. It was the same scene he'd heard when he and Ava had first entered the house. Auntie had paused the video. "You were spying on us."

Auntie shrugged unashamed. "So when are you going to tell Ava you're in love with her?"

Dai sipped his drink and kept his gaze on the screen.

Auntie grinned, amused.

"I'd never jeopardize what we have," he finally said.

She shrugged. "If you say so." The moment Ava returned, Auntie fixed her fingers into the shape of a heart and said, "Love," in Korean.

Dai quickly gathered up the dishes and headed to the kitchen. Ava followed him. "What was that about?"

He set the dishes on the counter. "Nothing."

"I'm glad you don't mind humoring her."

"It's okay," he grumbled then returned to the living room.

Ava remembered the first time Auntie had called him Korean and she'd asked if he was offended and he'd said people mixed up his ethnicity all the time and he preferred naiveté to racial slurs.

When she went into the living room she saw Donovan had removed his headphones and was patting a happy Felix, but when she looked at Dai she had a sense he was avoiding her gaze.

"We'd better go," he said, with his back to her as he gathered Donovan's things and put them into his backpack. "I'll drop you off—"

"No, it's out of your way. I'll get a ride. I'm not leaving just yet."

"Or you can spend the night," Donovan said. "I can tell you about—"

Ava sent an uncertain look at Dai. "Another time."

"But we miss you. You haven't—"

She knelt in front of him. "I know. It's been a busy summer. But you've been having fun at camp, right?"

Donovan folded his arms, ready to argue. "Yes, but—"

She stroked his head. "I'll see you before school starts. I'll help you pick out your school supplies. And new sneakers."

He stared up at his dad, delighted. "I'm getting new shoes?"

Dai sent Ava a look of amusement. "You are now."

He returned his gaze to Ava. "Can't it be sooner? You can—"

"Don't keep your dad waiting." Ava stood. "And I want to help Auntie with dinner before I go."

Donovan made a face but didn't argue. He and Dai said their goodbyes then headed for the foyer. Auntie waited to hear the front door close before she said, "When are you two going to stop pretending you're not in love with each other?"

Ava gathered the glasses and put them on the tray. "Of course I love him. We're friends."

"A butterfly does not return to its cocoon. Your love has already changed."

She didn't want to admit that she'd felt it too. "It's nothing."

"Is it because of your mother?"

Ava sat down and looked down at her hands. "Even if...what you were suggesting was even the tiniest bit true, and I'm not saying it is, but just if..." She took a deep breath. "...if I chose him, she'd never approve of him. She certainly wouldn't accept Donovan."

"No. But you can't make your parents happy in all things."

"I know but I can still try to make them happy in most things."

"Why?"

Because it was part of her identity. She was the good one. The sweet one. The one who didn't cause any trouble. She saw what had happened to Maya. She knew the same could happen to her. But more than that, she wanted to protect the role she had in Dai's life.

Friendship had kept her constantly by his side. A relationship would destroy that. She didn't want to be another woman who'd come and go in his life. As a friend she could be completely herself. A romantic relationship came with certain obligations and social pressures she wasn't ready to commit to again. Especially not with him.

She'd always been careful to choose the men she dated so that she could, not exactly manipulate but rather manage them. She wouldn't be able to do that with Dai. There were still sides to her she didn't want him to see.

Most of her friends were for show. People she used to show she had a social life, to show her parents she was making the right decisions, or people she could help. Dai was her only true friend.

Best to stay safe. Best to keep things as they were. He'd soon find someone else and so would she. "Nothing has changed."

"Pretending to be stupid doesn't help you either."

"I'm not pretending," Ava said stung by the criticism.

"Then if you're actually this stupid, I feel sorry for you. Change is always happening. The question is what do you do?

You either grow together or you grow apart. Nothing stays the same."

Ava looked down at her hands and rubbed them together. "He's my best friend. That will never change. He knows that."

"Then you will lose him."

She looked up sharply. "What?"

Auntie shook her head in pity. "Don't you see? Your hands are empty. You've already lost what you're trying to hold on to. In life things either grow, change or die. You make that choice or the choice will be made for you."

33

———

"Can I invite Sandy to come over?" Donovan asked his father as he put his dinner dishes in the sink.

"You just saw her."

"That was ages ago."

"That was three weeks ago."

"But she hasn't come over in a long time."

Dai didn't want to think about Ava's untouched slippers, the way she'd absently rearranged his condiments, how she always managed to find the dorkiest, sappiest family movie for all of them to watch.

It had been over a month since she'd visited the house, since Dai had kissed her outside his bedroom door.

Only weeks since she'd kissed him in the store...but it felt like a lifetime to Dai as well.

But they'd agreed that it was best for the charade that she kept her distance until summer camp was over. But Dai knew she was keeping her distance for another reason and he wouldn't force her. "No, not yet."

"Why not?"

Dai walked over to the sink and added more dishes. "Because I said so."

"Then can we visit her—"

"Let it go, Dynamo."

"But I want to see her. I miss her."

Dai took a deep breath feeling his patience thinning. "You just saw her," he repeated.

"Soooo long ago. I want to see her again."

"You'll see her another time."

"When?"

"I don't know. Another couple weeks. She's really busy right now."

"You let me see her all the time when you were with Ms. Cardoza."

"That was different."

"How come she didn't come home with us after seeing Auntie? She always comes home with us."

Dai gritted his teeth. "Not always and she explained she wanted to help Auntie with dinner."

"You usually do that and Auntie, Sandy and I—"

"That's enough," Dai said, his head starting to pound. He didn't need to be reminded of how things used to be. "Go play."

"Did you fight?"

"We're not talking about this anymore."

"But I want her to come over and it's been *forever*. I want to show her my new robot and what I found behind the gas station."

Dai turned on the faucet full blast. "She doesn't need to see that."

"She likes what I find."

Dai slammed the faucet off and spun around. "She doesn't need to see your garbage."

Tears sprung to his eyes, his lower lip trembled. "It's not

garbage," Donovan said in a quiet voice. "It's my treasure. And she understands that. She's the only one who does!" He stormed away, moments later a door slammed closed.

Dai sighed then swore. He hadn't handled that right. He'd been keeping his distance from Ava because that was how she wanted it, but he hadn't realized how much it had affected his son.

Dai walked upstairs and knocked on Donovan's door then opened it.

"I'm sorry," he said to the lump hidden under the blankets.

"It's not trash," Donovan said in a tear soaked voice.

"I know. That was wrong of me. It's not true."

"I want to see Sandy, please."

He hated that his son felt the need to beg. He sat down on the side of the bed. "I'll see if she's free this weekend."

Donovan's head popped out from under the covers. "Can I call her? Can I see if she's free? Can I tell her about my new puzzle? Oh and what about that dog that got hit by a—"

"No, you cannot tell her about that."

"Or that woman who showed you her boobs."

"Definitely not that," Dai said, remembering the incident with regret. Going against his better judgment, and desperate to get over his feelings for Ava, he'd let his cousin Koji set him up with his "friend."

They met for drinks at a classy bar. At first she seemed like the perfect diversion: A leggy, curvaceous brunette who moved like a model. She was smart, beautiful, funny, but after she downed six cocktails in less than an hour and twice attempted to grab his crotch, her charm wore off.

"Koji didn't tell me you were shy," she said when Dai moved her hand away.

He stood up from the bar stool. "We'd better go."

"Koji said I could do you a favor." She leaned into him,

pressing her soft body against his. "I can make you forget her. At least tonight."

He was tempted. Because he did want to forget. He wanted to forget all his feelings for a woman who wanted to push him away. He wanted to forget Elena's betrayal. He wanted to stop longing for what he couldn't have.

One night would be enough. Just sex. Nothing complicated. No promises made. No promises broken. Just a primal itch relieved at the hands of a woman who found him attractive.

She was nothing like Ava. He could give her the night. Donovan was with his mother, if he promised to donate to one of her favorite causes, she'd understand.

But to his annoyance he took the coward's way out and said,

"Not tonight."

He should have said 'no' because since then she hoped to hook up again. He gently tried to tell her he wasn't interested, but she still didn't get the hint and eventually sent him nude photos of herself lounging in a hotel room in the Bahamas with a caption saying, *See what you're missing.*

Dai had been looking at the photos on his cell phone not knowing that Donovan had been looking over his shoulder until his son said, "How come she's doing that with her boobs?"

Dai had been so startled by the sudden question he'd tossed the phone as if he were a criminal getting rid of stolen loot.

"Is she your new girlfriend?"

"No. She's a model," Dai lied and distracted his son with ice cream, but unfortunately Donovan hadn't forgotten the incident. He looked at his son's curious expression and kept his voice firm. "You are not to tell anyone about that. Clear?" he sighed when Donovan suddenly looked guilty. "You already told someone?"

"Just my friend. He laughed."

"Fine, that's done, but nobody else can know."

"Not even Sandy?"

"Definitely not Sandy. Understood?"

Donovan nodded. "Can I call her now?"

"It's late. You can call her tomorrow."

"It's not that late."

"You're not calling her now."

Donovan jumped out of bed fully recovered. He spread his arms wide and spun around in a circle. "I can't wait to talk to her. I hope she can spend the whole day with us. Oh, I'll have to see if we have enough nkate cake. I think I ate the last one. Can we get more?"

The sweet, crunchy Ghanaian treat of roasted peanuts was one of Donovan and Ava's favorites. Watching them devour the square confection always made him smile. "Yes."

"It's so much fun when she's with us. I love her so much. You love her too, don't you Dad?"

"Go and see if we have enough nkate cake."

Donovan dashed out of the room.

Dai shoved his hands in his pockets and sighed. "And yeah, I love her too."

34

———

But Donovan didn't get a chance to call Ava the next day. Instead he came down with a severe cold that Dai caught soon after, which left them both weak and miserable.

When the doorbell rang on the third day of the cold-that-felt-like-he'd-been-scorched-by-a-fire-breathing monster, it rang in Dai's head like the gong of a church bell. He shuffled to the door and opened it, squinting against the bright light of the sun.

At first he didn't recognize the dark figure with sunglasses and a black face mask, until they spoke. "Your mother hadn't heard from you and got worried so she called me," Ava said. "So when I called—"

"You called?" he croaked, his mouth as dry as sandpaper.

"And Donovan told me you were both sick I decided to bring reinforcements." She held up a cooler.

"You shouldn't be here. The place is a mess."

"I didn't come here as a guest." She stepped in and closed the door, descending into the dimness of the few lights he had on. He hadn't realized how dark the house was until then. He couldn't remember the last time he'd opened the blinds.

Ava pushed past him. "Go and lie down." She took off her sunglasses and slipped out of her shoes. "You look awful."

"I feel worse."

"Yeah," Donovan said, popping up behind him. "He fainted twice."

Dai shuffled back to the couch, too tired to remove the take-away cartons from last night that littered the coffee table. "I didn't faint. I stood up too fast and sort of fell down."

"You were probably dehydrated," Ava said. "You're still sweating."

Dai tugged on the T-shirt plastered to his skin. He probably smelled too. This was not how he wanted her to see him. He waved her away. "Thanks for stopping by. Leave the cooler."

Donovan circled Ava like an excited puppy. "The second time Dad hit the floor so hard I thought he was dead."

Dai sank down into the couch. "That's enough, Dynamo."

"His head hit my Legos spaceship and smashed it." Donovan spread his arms out to the side. "Pieces flew everywhere."

"I already apologized about that."

"And blood gushed from his head."

"That's an exaggeration," Dai said when Ava glanced at the bandage on his forehead. "A minor cut."

"And he wasn't moving."

"Dynamo—"

"But at least he was breathing."

"Yes," Ava said with a gentle laugh sensing Dai's discomfort. "I'm glad he's okay."

"He's not. But I am though." Donovan took her hand. "I'm so glad you're here. We missed you. Now I can show what I did with the crank I found at the junkyard."

Dai frowned. "Junkyard? When did you go to a junkyard?"

For a moment Donovan looked panicked, which was odd. He stared at his father speechless, which was stranger still.

"Probably a school trip," Ava said filling the silence.

Donovan nodded quickly. "Yes, that's right."

"Hmm, I don't remember giving permission for that." But then again his head felt too foggy to remember a lot of things.

"You did, you said it was okay."

"When did you—"

"Have you eaten anything?" Ava asked as if she wanted to change the subject. If Dai hadn't felt so tired he would have wondered why, but at that moment he didn't think much of it. Instead he started to reply but his son beat him to it.

"I did but he didn't." Donovan cupped his mouth and said in a stage whisper, "Dad always stops eating and gets angry when he's sick."

"I'm not angry," Dai said, sounding exactly that.

"Let's go warm up some rice porridge then," Ava said, taking Donovan's hand.

"Don't bother, I'm not hungry," Dai said.

But the moment Ava presented him with rice porridge garnished with salted salmon and nori, Dai consumed the mild, light meal like a starving man.

"This doesn't taste like the one I made," Dai mumbled around a large spoonful.

"It's not," Ava said, opening a window. "I got some help from your mother."

"Grandma's better," Donovan said eating his bowl while sitting at the coffee table Ava had cleaned. Dai was actually surprised his mother hadn't come by yet since she was only a half hour away.

"Sure," he said in good humor, used to his son's honesty. "Kick a man when he's down." He glanced down when his cell phone alerted him to a text. Speak of the devil it was from his mother.

> Mom: I'm sending Ava over with some porridge.
>
> Dai: She's already here.
>
> Mom: Good. I thought you'd want her more than me. Auntie wishes you well.

Dai silently groaned at the rolling on the floor laughing emoji she added. He wasn't sure if his mother didn't know what the emoji meant or if she really thought his situation was hilarious. But one thing was certain: Auntie had called his mother and they were determined to play matchmaker while Ava stayed blissfully unaware of their ulterior motives.

But he wouldn't let their nosy efforts sour his mood. He finished the nourishing and healthy meal, feeling comforted and cared for, remembering when his mother had done the same when he'd been sick as a child. He set his spoon down with a satisfied sigh. "Thanks." He rested his head back barely able to keep his eyes open. "You don't have to do anymore. We can take care of the dishes."

"Go to bed," Ava said, opening another window. "It's okay."

He didn't argue, glad someone was there to look after Donovan. Dai slowly rose to his feet and barely made it upstairs before collapsing on his bed.

He woke up to darkness.

But at least he no longer felt like death. Dai sat up, rubbed his cheek (damn when was the last time he shaved?) and stumbled to his bedroom door.

He wasn't used to this kind of quiet. Donovan was rarely quiet. Even when he was keeping himself busy he was whistling or humming.

Silence and Donovan usually spelled trouble.

Dai rushed into the hallway ready to barrel down the stairs pleased that he didn't smell smoke or paint fumes or something acidic and stopped when he noticed Donovan's bedroom door ajar. For some reason his son didn't like his door closed.

Dai carefully pushed it open and saw the bed empty. It was late. If Donovan wasn't in bed...

Dai's heartbeat raced as he hurried down the stairs. The sound of murmured voices floated from the living room.

He stood in the entryway and swept the room lit only by one lamplight and tried to take in what he saw. The Lego spaceship stood partially rebuilt, crumbs had been vacuumed from the area rug, the room smelled fresh. Then he saw Donovan fast asleep, his head resting on Ava's lap.

He didn't expect to see her still there. He thought she might put Donovan to bed then quietly leave.

But here she was.

And it had never felt more right.

Ava turned to him and pressed a finger to her lips before pointing to Donovan.

Dai could only stare as she carefully shifted out from under Donovan and gently placed the child's head on the sofa without waking him.

Dai gripped his fist, a wave of emotions flooded him. This is what he wanted. This was home to him. *She* was home to him. He wanted to win her. He wanted her to be his.

A fierce desire to claim her, grabbed him even tighter than his fever had. His skin felt hot, his heart hammered in his chest. He loved her. She was the only one for him.

The strength of that realization made his head spin.

He took a step forward but his legs gave way and he grabbed the back of a chair before he crumbled to the ground.

Ava rushed over to support him. "You should have stayed in

bed."

Dai closed his eyes, feeling the light pressure of her hand on his back, the soft touch of her fingers against his neck, the gentle scent of her lotion that reminded him of summer cantaloupe and honeydew. She had no idea the power she had over him. He rubbed his forehead and forced himself to stand taller. He would win her but not like this. "I need to take a shower."

She grabbed his arm. "No, you're not strong enough."

"I'll be fine," he said, trying to ease the worry in her eyes. "Trust me."

"Have some ginger tea first."

"No, I—"

"You either sit and have ginger tea or I wake Donovan up."

It was a powerful threat. Donovan could sleep through a rocket launch, but the moment he was awake, getting him back to sleep would be a nightmare. Dai reluctantly sat down. "You have a mean streak."

Ava patted him on the shoulder and said in a bright, superior voice. "You should know that by now."

Dai scowled his way through the ginger tea, not wanting to admit he found the ginger and honey soothing, then raced upstairs and took a shower and shaved.

He pulled on a pair of jeans and was shuffling through his T-shirts when the doubts began to build. *There's no way you could win Ava. Why would she want you anyway? Do you think she liked looking after you and Donovan? Why would she want to be part of this chaos? She could find a man without a kid and an ex. Someone her family would approve of. You could ruin the best thing that's ever happened to you.*

Dai grabbed a T-shirt and slammed the closet door shut. He didn't care. Loving Ava felt right. It would take time but he'd convince her that she loved him too.

35

He returned to the living room wearing a pair of jeans and a clean T-shirt.

"Sit down and I'll get you something to eat," Ava said.

He frowned. "Didn't I just eat?"

"You had tea, but you haven't eaten in hours. Do you want more porridge or something else?"

"Porridge is fine, but I can get it—"

"Sit down, Dai. I'll be right back."

He swore. God this was killing him. He didn't want her to treat him like a patient. He looked around the room wondering what he could help her with, but the space was spotless. Of course she'd closed the blinds. He glanced at the TV and shook his head. Hell she'd even dusted.

"Didn't I tell you to sit down?"

Dai spun around and saw Ava holding a tray. He rubbed his hands on his jeans like a kid caught in the hallway by the principle. "Yes."

She motioned to the sofa with a jerk of her chin.

Dai sat and cleared his throat. "Thanks for all this. If you'd come a couple days later the housekeeper would have cleaned up," he said, wanting her to know that life with him wouldn't be a drudgery. He could afford things now, but that would make little difference to her because she'd grown up with a housekeeper. It was expected, not an added bonus. The problem was he didn't know how to impress her, she already knew too much about him. She knew his father was wealthy, but not a major part of his life, that his mother still worked passionately at a non-profit helping the less fortunate and had enough rally and protest buttons to sink a canoe; that Dai's business made more in an hour than she earned in a year, but that he'd never flaunt it...

Ava clicked her tongue in sympathy. "If you want to go back to bed I can carry this upstairs."

Dai sat back and looked up at her, forcing a smile. "No, really. I'm not tired."

"You still look exhausted."

Her words deflated him like a grounded air balloon. The shower and shave hadn't made a difference to her. Clearly he wouldn't be changing her mind about him tonight.

She set the tray on his lap then picked up the spoon. "Want me to feed you?"

He glared at her and snatched the spoon from her. "Very funny."

She laughed softly then said, "Need me to change your bandage?"

"I'm fine."

"I wasn't sure, considering the blood I had to clean off the floor."

He swore and stared at her alarmed. "Really?"

Ava covered her mouth and giggled. "No, not really. Lighten up, Dai."

He shot her a glance. "I will get you back for that."

She took a seat in the armchair, and flashed a sly grin. "You can try."

He took a spoonful of porridge and bit back a moan of pleasure. It was so good. "I hope he didn't cause you too much trouble."

"He's fine. We know each other."

Dai felt relieved. He never had to worry about Donovan with her. Ava understood him. She could take his wild imagination and energy; she had dealt with his screaming fits when he was a toddler. Dai was glad his son had passed that stage, but he knew there was so much more ahead and most times he wasn't sure he had what it took to face them. But with Ava...

With her he always felt as if things would be okay. That no matter how bad things got he could manage because she believed in him.

She pressed her hand to his forehead. "Stop that," he said.

"I'm checking to see if you still have a temperature."

"I don't. I don't need a nurse either."

She made a face. "No need to be miserable."

"Sit down. You're making me feel nervous."

"Why?"

"Do I look like I'm going to die?"

"No."

"Then stop looking at me as if death is knocking at the door."

"But you look—"

He felt his cheeks heat. "Stop talking about how I look. I'm feeling better."

"I was worried about you."

"It's a stupid cold."

She cleared her throat. "I'm sorry about what I said at Auntie's."

He wondered if she still thought he was on the rebound,

but he'd handle it later. "It's okay. I'm glad you came. It's late. You can stay in the guest bedroom." He stood.

"Actually I—"

"Otherwise I wake this little monster up and tell him you're coming by tomorrow too."

"That's just mean."

"I learned from the best." Dai chuckled. "Let me take him upstairs. Don't go anywhere."

"Are you sure you're strong enough?"

"Yes. Even if I drop him he won't wake up."

Ava frowned. "That's not funny."

Dai smiled. "What? You think you're the only one who can tell bad jokes?"

"My joke wasn't bad."

"Relax. I won't drop him." He winked. "But if you don't believe me, I can practice with you first."

36

———

SHE'D LIED. Dai didn't look exhausted. When he'd returned to the living room, freshly showered and shaved, he looked at her in a new way. A way that made her notice the way his shirt stretched across his chest, the shape of his thighs, his mouth. And now he was flirting with her and waiting for a response.

She glanced at Donovan, bit her lip and decided to take a risk. "If you weren't contagious, I'd let you."

He narrowed his eyes. She knew he was considering his response. He wasn't as good a verbal banter as she was. "Don't toy with me, Ava."

"You started it."

"But I wasn't joking."

"Me either. Such a shame you have a cold otherwise..."

"I won't be contagious in a week."

"Are you asking for a rain check?"

He leaned forward, rested his elbows on his knees and shook his head. "I'm not asking, I'm setting a date."

"Okay. I'll reserve a hotel room."

His gaze clung to hers. "You won't need to. Donovan will be with his mother."

She resisted the urge to look away. He'd offered her a challenge and she would face it. "Okay, I'll see you then."

But one phone call would change their plans.

When Ava stopped by a few days later to give Donovan and Dai some sweets Auntie had made, the look on Dai's face when he opened the door as well as the way he gripped his cell phone to his chest, let her know something was wrong.

She could always tell when Dai was on the phone with his ex. Some men might look angry or annoyed. Dai always looked devastated.

He motioned Ava forward then returned the phone to his ear. "But we agreed that you— Of course I'm shouting! We talked about this months ago. He's looking forward to it! Okay...okay...I'm not shouting now. But this isn't fair... I *am* listening."

Ava set the sweets on the kitchen counter and returned to the living room where Dai paced.

"Right," he said. "That doesn't change...What? This is not what we planned. Where are you going?" he demanded as Ava crept to the front door. "No, I'm not talking to you," he said to his ex then glared at Ava and pointed at the armchair.

She held up her hands and shook her head then motioned to the door.

Dai pointed again with more force.

Ava backed up and sunk into the chair.

"Yes, I'm still here," Dai said, pacing again. "Where else would I be? What? Yes, Ava's here. No, you're not going to talk to her...Because this isn't about her. I don't need her to talk sense. I'm not being unreasonable. Do they know what he's like? No, I'm not being selfish, I'm looking out for him... I know he's your son too but... Fine, fine. Yes, I understand. Okay." He disconnected then threw the phone at the couch.

Ava cautiously rose to her feet. "Um, Dai?"

Dai picked up the phone, gripped it in his fist and pounded a seat cushion then stood and threw it at the sofa again. "She always does this. We plan something and at the last minute. The very last minute she cancels or changes things!

"Donovan was supposed to spend a week with her, now she wants him to spend time with her family in Jamaica. She says her mother really wants to see him. Her brother, the one who lives in New York, will come and meet us at the airport and fly with him." He made a fist. "She always out maneuvers me. She doesn't give me a chance to stop her. She knows I've pulled him out of summer camp early so that he can spend time with her, that there's a week before school starts again. I know I could reinstate him in the program but then she'd accuse me of monopolizing our son and remind me of how much she's trying."

He laughed bitterly. "And boy has she tried. She's already bought the tickets, made travel plans. I can't argue that he was going to spend time with her anyway, that she has a right to alter how she was going to look after him. I'd already had most of his things packed but..."

He collapsed into the sofa. "I can try to protect him from so many things, but I can't protect him from her."

Ava sat down beside him. "I met her mother at the wedding and she seemed very nice. And we've both met her brother a few times when you two were still married. Donovan is okay with him so he's not traveling with a stranger and her brother seems responsible. I don't think she'd put her son at risk."

Dai sighed. "I know. But he's going to be disappointed."

"I probably should go before you tell him."

Dai rested his head back. "It might sound better coming from you."

"I don't think so."

Dai swore. "He's happily playing in his room right now and because of her I have to..."

"I know. I'm sorry."

Dai swore again then sat up. "Might as well get it over with."

Ava headed to the door.

"You don't have to go."

"I think this should be private between you two," Ava said, putting on her shoes. "Tell him about the sweets and that I'll see him off at the airport. It might give him something to look forward to."

Dai nodded, resting his hands on his hips. "You're right. It might be harder with you here. Maybe he won't take it so hard."

37

———————

Donovan erupted in outrage.

"But I don't want to go to Jamaica!" He jumped up from the sofa, where he and Dai had been sitting, and stomped the length of the living room. "It's not fair!"

Dai remained seated. "Your uncle's going to fly with you and your grandmother wants to see you, plus you can play with your cousins."

Donovan glared at him, his eyes shimmering with tears. "You said I was going to be with Mom."

Dai rubbed his neck, hearing the hurt in his son's voice. "I know, but something came up. She said she'll try to visit you there."

"But I don't want to go. I want to stay here with you." He jumped on the couch and shifted over to Dai, crawling on his knees. "I'll be good. I promise. Please."

"It's not about you being good."

He wrapped his hands around Dai's arm. "Don't send me away, Dad."

"I'm not sending you away," he snapped then softened his

tone. "This will be good for you. You can go to the beach and you'll have so much to do, you'll be back here before you know it."

Donovan's hands fell to his side and he hung his head. "Okay," he said in a quiet voice of defeat.

BUT IT WASN'T OKAY. At the airport when he saw his uncle waiting for him at the passenger-only entrance, Donovan began to cry. He looked up at Dai and said, "Do I really have to go?"

"Yes." Dai nudged him forward. He'd already spoken to his former brother-in-law on the phone and peppered him with questions that only calmed him a little. Not because he didn't trust him, but because he felt helpless. They'd agreed that they'd keep their distance for Donovan's sake. "Go on."

Donovan hung his head and cried harder.

Ava saw Dai's eyes flash and his jaw twitch. He was just as upset as his son but trying not to show it.

She took Donovan's hand. "Let's walk for a minute."

Donovan hiccuped, wiped his eyes and let her lead him away. Ava tried to ignore the curious looks sent their way, hoping he wouldn't start crying again since he looked older than seven and could appear like a spoiled child throwing a tantrum to untrained eyes.

She stopped in front of a kiosk then knelt in front of him.

"I need you to be brave. This is very hard for your Dad."

Donovan's eyes refilled with tears. "He's sending me away."

"No, he wants you to be with your family. He didn't get a chance like this when he was young."

"But I don't want it."

"But what about the treasures?"

He paused. "The treasures?"

"Yes. All that you can discover on this amazing island will be incredible."

"Better than the junkyard?"

Ava hesitated not thinking it was a fair comparison. But if Donovan thought the junkyard was a wondrous place she wouldn't argue. "It's much, much better. You can find lots of treasures and take pictures to show me. You're an adventurer, aren't you?"

"Yes."

"Then adventurers have to leave home and explore, but they always know they have a home to come back to. Besides, this trip won't be as long as you think. Soon you'll be back here and we'll see each other again." She wiped his face. "So no more crying."

"What if they don't like me?"

"If anyone is mean to you, you can call me anytime and let me know and I'll do something about it."

"Promise?"

Ava hugged him. "I promise."

Donovan hugged her back, his arms wrapped tight around her neck. "I love you, Sandy."

"I love you too." Ava blinked back tears then quickly stood up. "Let's go."

They were a few yards away when they saw Dai standing with his arms folded, looking fierce.

"Dad looks mad."

"Because he's sad to see you go."

Donovan looked up at her surprised. "Really?"

"Yes, really. So you have to let him know you'll be okay. Can you do that?"

Donovan raced over to Dai and grabbed his suitcase. He looked up at his father. "I'm ready to go now. I'm alright. I'll be good."

Dai nodded stiffly and patted Donovan on the back when his son hugged him. "Go on," he said his voice sounding rougher than he'd meant it to.

Dai watched Donovan walk over to his uncle. He turned just as his son was waving goodbye, so Ava smiled and waved for him.

Dai was halfway near the exits when she finally caught up with him.

"He's going to be fine," she said.

He didn't respond. He didn't argue when she offered to drive.

He stayed silent on the drive back.

It was hard to let him go. He knew it was good for Donovan to know the other side of his family. A chance Dai hadn't had. His paternal grandparents showed little interest in him. He'd been to Ghana twice. Once in his early twenties when his father had invited him to attend a wedding for an uncle, he'd felt like an outsider and had been treated as one; and again when his grandfather had died. He'd gotten a chance to meet half-siblings who were nearly two decades younger and extended family who felt like strangers. His maternal grandparents were cordial but didn't always understand their youngest daughter's radical ways so he didn't get to know much about them either.

He'd wanted more for his son. At least his former in-laws tried to make an effort to know Donovan while his ex kept her distance.

This was good for him.

But it still hurt.

He already missed him.

The car turned onto the long driveway leading up to his house sooner than he'd expected. He followed Ava to the front door, dreading how quiet the house would be. How empty it would feel.

Ava unlocked the door and opened it. "You did the right thing."

He shuffled through the door not sure he believed her, but glad she'd said it all the same.

"I'll stay until I hear they've landed."

He felt the tightness in his chest ease a little. She'd taken time off that Friday to be with him and now would stay without him asking her to, he could have kissed her for that. He kicked off his shoes. Who was he fooling? He wanted to kiss her anyway. He didn't need a reason.

"You probably should go," he whispered, his voice raw and vulnerable.

She patted him on the back. "You should go and take a shower. It will help you relax."

It would. It usually did. It would help clear his head.

But as the shower's hot water quickly steamed up the mirror and sliding glass door, he wasn't sure it would help.

He sighed and briefly closed his eyes.

When he opened them his body froze.

38

———

Oh. My. God. He'd started to hallucinate. He'd started hallucinating about a towel clad Ava wearing a pink shower cap, walking into the bathroom and then closing the door behind her.

He'd conjured up a vision of Ava slowly stripping the dark blue towel off her smooth brown body and opening the glass door.

Stepping into the shower with him.

Touching his face.

Pressing her soft, wet lips against his.

At first he didn't move, afraid that if he did, this beautiful illusion would disappear.

But her kiss was too light, too tame. He wanted more.

Dai wrapped his arms around her sleek body and drew her closer, deepening the kiss. He drank in the sweetness of her mouth, making her moan.

This was no dream, this was amazingly real.

He felt the spray of water cascading over them, the sound of it hitting the tile, but it could not drown out the pounding of his heart. *Ava. Sweetest, Ava.* His hands greedily slid over her wet body not wanting to miss any inch of it.

She pulled away and said, "Dai—"

But he kissed her words away. *No don't speak. Not now.*

He cut the shower off with his fist. The abrupt act seemed to startle her at first then she met his gaze and understood.

He turned off the water as she left the shower and grabbed a towel. He grabbed her around the waist and drew her against him.

She laughed. "Dai, I'm all wet."

"I know," he said in a deep tone, making it clear that he liked it.

She slipped out of his grasp. "You'll catch a cold again." She wrapped the towel around herself.

"No, I won't." She let out a shriek of alarm when he lifted her up in his arms. He met her startled gaze with a smoldering dark look. "Don't worry I won't drop you."

She wrapped her arms around his neck then nipped at his ear before touching it with the tip of her tongue.

For a second his grip loosened. He swore and adjusted his hold on her. "Except if you do that I might."

"Then you'd better start moving."

He'd never moved so fast. He dropped her on his king size bed and she bounced up and down, her laughter filling the room.

He knew he'd wanted her, but until this moment he hadn't realized how much.

His body covered hers; she pressed her open lips to his.

His hands explored the soft lines of her body with aching tenderness.

Here there was no need for words. He could be her equal.

Here the world was theirs, there was nothing to separate them. With every touch he made sure she knew that.

Ava knew Dai was a passionate man, but the depth of his desire shocked her. For a man usually in constant motion he took his time. She'd seen him like this once when he was still working at the mechanic's shop and he'd been working on a classic Mustang. She'd remembered the way his hand cradled the side mirror, slid over the wheels, slowly glided over the hood, the awe and reverence of his gaze.

He rolled on a condom and glided inside her like she was a turbo charged sports car he wanted to ride at high speed.

As if she'd become a new obsession.

He held nothing back.

But Ava still remained guarded.

Sex had been enjoyable in a purely perfunctory way. She enjoyed it because she was supposed to not because she actually found it enjoyable.

But with Dai...ohhhhh. She arched into him wanting to fill every crevice of his hot, hard body with her own.

She bit back a gasp, drowning in an ocean of sweet ecstasy. Who knew it could be this way?

He shifted inside her and she cried out in surprised delight, feeling as if she'd shatter into pieces, then shrunk back in shame at her animalistic response, but Dai smiled, his dark, heated gaze making it clear he wanted more.

She had nothing to be ashamed of. She could be herself. She bit her lip, feeling wild and free.

He was someone she could please without suppressing her own desires.

So she surrendered and he responded to her without a need for words. They knew each other, with a look, with a glance, with a moan, their bodies moved in harmony. They were in sync soaring together on the wings of ecstasy until they finally collapsed exhausted, their heavy breathing filling the silence.

The sound of a light chime floated through the air.

Dai fumbled for his cell phone, which he'd left on the side table before taking a shower. He quickly read the text then set the phone down.

"They've arrived safely," he said.

Ava affectionately patted his chest before she sat up. "Then my job is done."

He wrapped an arm around her waist, stopping her from leaving. "You know you're more than a distraction." He held her tighter. He sat up and pressed a kiss on the curve of her neck. "Stay."

She turned fully to him and gently pushed him onto his back, before trailing a finger down his chest. "You'd still make a beautiful nude," she said reminding him of what she'd first said when they'd met.

"Don't tease me."

"I'm not teasing." She lifted up the blanket and stared at the rest of him. "I can see why Elena was so impressed."

Dai pulled her down on top of him, wrapped his arms around her, holding her still. "I'm not going to let you avoid the subject."

Ava grinned. "I'm not avoiding anything."

"Then you'll stay."

"I guess one night won't hurt."

He kissed her then whispered against her lips. "I want six."

Ava scrambled out of his grasp and sat up. "You want six nights?"

"Yes."

She reached for the towel that had been discarded on the floor.

He groaned. "Come on, don't do that."

She sent him a look then tossed the towel and slipped under the covers. She lay on her side and faced him.

"Dai, this was just—"

He pressed a finger to her lips. "I'm tired of pretending, Ava. We both know this wasn't a fling. I didn't sleep with you because I miss my son and you didn't sleep with me because you're worried about me being alone. Admit it. You wanted this as much as I did."

Ava gathered up the sheets to her chest and fell on her back. Staring up at the ceiling was easier than looking at him. She wasn't ready to admit to anything yet.

"If I stay here my commute will be longer."

Dai told her another route that would make it shorter.

She felt him move closer before he said, "What are you scared of Ava?"

Me, she wanted to tell him. I'm scared of me. Scared at what a new relationship with him would reveal about herself. He wasn't someone she could manipulate; he could peel away the layers of the façade she still kept closely guarded.

And yet a part of her didn't care.

A part of her wanted to risk it all. She'd already surrendered to a dangerous temptation. She wasn't ready to stop now.

But she had to be strategic. She turned to him.

This man beside her, with the intense, probing gaze, and touch that could make her body tingle, was someone completely new and unfamiliar. And yet...she felt she'd known him all her life.

Dai. Her heart sang his name. Being with him made her happy.

What are you afraid of Ava?

She wouldn't be afraid. She wouldn't lose this chance.

She'd cherish these seven days with him.

She smiled and touched his cheek, easing the furrow in his brow.

"Nothing. Nothing at all."

39

"Where are you going?" her mother demanded when she saw Ava's valise bag in the foyer.

"It's a business trip," Ava said heading back upstairs.

Her mother blocked her path. "You didn't tell us about this. What's it for? Where is it? What's your itinerary?"

"Leave her be," her father said walking through the foyer to go to the family room.

"She could be visiting the fiancé that doesn't exist."

"She explained that there'd been a misunderstanding and she hadn't wanted to correct the woman you'd met at the store. Don't fault her for having good manners. She's always taken the feelings of others into account."

Her mother frowned. "Yes, I suppose. But where will you be?"

"It's just in another county," Ava said. "But I wanted to stay in the hotel."

"Which county? What is the name of the hotel?"

"I'll let you know," she said darting around her. "I really

have to finish packing. There's a colleague I want to meet up with." She raced up the stairs and walked into her room.

She halted when she saw Cat sitting on her bed, sucking a lollipop. "What kind of business trip needs this?" Cat pulled out something hidden behind her back and held up a pair of black lace panties.

Ava snatched them from her and shoved them back in her suitcase. "None of your business."

"Is it Dai's business?"

Ava felt her cheeks burn. "Donovan's in Jamaica and he's feeling a little lost and I want to be there for him."

"And on top of him. Wrapped around him."

"Stop that. We're just going to have some fun."

Cat rolled the lollipop against her tongue turning it extra red before she said, "Sure, tell yourself that."

"It's true."

"Why can't you just admit how you feel about him?"

Ava carefully added two blouses. "It's too soon."

Cat rolled her eyes. "Because nearly twenty years is just not enough."

"It hasn't been twenty years."

"At the rate you're going it will be."

Ava nudged her sister with her foot. "What are you doing in here anyway? Shouldn't you be running errands or terrifying men."

They both found Cat's affect on Keeden's friend, Bryant, amusing. When they visited his friend Keeden he managed to disappear every time.

"I finished all my errands and Bryant's no longer at Keeden's house. Pity."

"You like terrifying him, don't you?"

"It's not on purpose."

Ava couldn't stop a smile. "He disappears the moment you enter a room, he shivers when he hears your name."

Cat grinned in response. "It's true, I rather like that."

Ava considered her sister for a moment. "Do you like him?"

A thoughtful look crossed her face. "At least I'm not invisible to him like I am to most people."

A strange non-answer.

"He's not what he seems." Cat leaped to her feet. "And neither are we." She pointed her lollipop at Ava her expression turning serious. "Don't underestimate Dai. I know you're afraid to be completely real with him, but he's stronger than you think."

Swish, swish, swish.

Ava sat at the kitchen table and watched Dai, enjoying the movement of his shoulders as he cleaned the rice. Coming here after work had become an easy routine. He was usually home before her and prepared the dinner. Today she'd come home early to catch him in the act. He'd given the cook the week off, since he'd planned to be alone for the week and didn't mind jumping in and doing the cooking.

She cupped her chin in her hand and watched him put the rice in the rice cooker then check the curried chicken he had simmering on the stove. He hummed as he pulled a cucumber from the refrigerator and grabbed a knife.

Chop, chop, chop.

Every night had been sublime.

Every morning a dream.

She remembered the first day she'd arrived, standing outside a door she'd passed through many times before, with her heart racing, wondering if things would now be awkward between them. She knew him to be a wonderful lover, but how would they be outside the bedroom?

She swallowed and knocked on the front door.

It swung open and all fear slipped away when she saw the scowl on his face. He was still Dai.

He looked big, sexy and a little mean. "What took you so long?" he said annoyed.

"I had to get past my mother."

He took her valise and suitcase with a jerk of impatience.

She lifted the two shopping bags she'd brought with her and stepped inside. "Plus, I sent you a text that I had to run errands."

Dai closed the door. "That was nearly two hours ago," he mumbled sounding as petulant as Donovan.

"Because I was getting something for you," she said, putting on her slippers.

"For me?"

She lifted the two shopping bags. "I plan to make you jollof rice and spicy cod. And a surprise dessert."

"You mean you finally figured out how to make a proper jollof rice?"

Ava stuck her tongue out at him.

Dai laughed. They'd always teased each other on whether Ghanaians or Nigerians made better jollof rice.

But the hot, burning kiss that followed his teasing was like nothing they'd shared before.

Ava had barely recovered from the sensual assault, when he took the bags from her and said, "You can cook tomorrow. I already have something planned for tonight." He motioned to the living room. "Go on in. I'll be right there," he said before he headed to the kitchen.

Ava took a moment to steady her heart and recover her breathing before she stepped into the living room.

She stopped in shock.

Dai had rearranged the room. He'd laid out a large picnic blanket and created a pillow crash pad in front of the TV.

Ava laughed amused at the assortment of snacks. "What's all this?"

Dai returned to the room and eagerly sat down. He turned on the TV and selected a movie. "I've always wanted to do this with you."

"But we've watched movies together all the time."

He pulled her down next to him and gathered her close. His dark gaze drank in the sight of her. "Not like this," he said in a low voice.

She pressed her lips against his, because he made lying to her mother worth it, then sank into the comfortable heat of his body before she rested her head on his shoulder and sighed. "You're right, not like this."

"It's the first thing I can cross off my list."

Ava lifted her head and looked at him curious. "You have a list?"

"Yes." Dai picked up his cell phone that he had at his side and showed her the list he'd typed there.

She quickly read through some of the items. "Late night dinner, sightseeing, amusement park, visit Grenada, see Mount Fuji..." She scrolled through the list amazed by the length of it. "Dai, you must have fifty items here."

"Two hundred actually, but I had to stop myself."

"Two hundred?"

"Don't worry. It wasn't easy, but I was able to cut it down to the top ten." He pointed to the screen. "See? I circled them in red."

"We can't do all this in seven days."

The corner of his mouth lifted in a quick grin. "Is that a challenge?"

He impressed her by how much he could pack into a weekend. They went sightseeing around DC, had a late night dinner at an exclusive restaurant a friend of Ava's had raved about, went paddleboating and on a scenic bike ride.

And he turned ordinary weekdays into mini-adventures. Things they'd done together hundreds of times before, like grocery shopping, walking in the park, cooking together, felt suddenly new. They held hands, cuddled, he was very affectionate stealing kisses, offering gentle caresses that always left her wanting more.

Then there had been the gifts.

The flowers that arrived at her office; the ruby bracelet her gave her at lunch; the emerald pendant necklace he'd left on her pillow one evening.

"You're spoiling me," Ava said lifting up the necklace in awe.

Dai stretched out on his side with a satisfied grin. "It's on my list."

Chop, chop, chop.

Ava stared at him cooking now, feeling warm and at home. It felt natural to be with him. It had been five days of heaven. She didn't want it to end. They'd fallen into an easy domesticity.

"So when do we get married?" she said.

The chopping stopped. Dai became very still.

That's when she realized she'd said the wrong thing. She shouldn't have teased him.

He spun around. His eyes met hers. "It'll have to be small because Donovan—"

"Gets overexcited in large crowds," she finished.

His face split into a wide grin and the joy in his eyes made her heart sink. "How about next fall?" He leaned back. "When do you want to move in? I can turn one of the guest bedrooms into a study for you." He rubbed his chin, thoughtful. "I already know the ring I'll buy you. No, better yet, I'll have you choose."

"Wait, don't get ahead of yourself."

He snapped his fingers. "Oh and we'll need more plates—"

"You need to slow down," Ava said.

"And I'll—"

"Dai, it's too soon!"

He blinked. "For what? We've got a lot of things to think about."

She bit her lip.

He folded his arms.

Tension filled the air.

Dai finally nodded. A look of hurt came and went. "Oh, I get it. It was a joke, right?"

"No," she lied because at that moment she wanted it to be true.

He hung his head and motioned her to him.

She cautiously did. "What is it?"

He gathered her close, relieved. "Forgive me for doubting you." He kissed her then his tender, heartfelt gaze met hers. "I'm sorry."

Ava wrapped her arms around his neck and hugged him so that he wouldn't see her blinking back tears.

40

———

Cᴀᴛ sᴛᴀʀᴇᴅ at her sister as if she'd suddenly sprouted wings.

"What do you mean you *accidentally* proposed to him?"

Ava groaned as she and Cat drove to a local donation drop off. Cat had been given the task to pack up and donate the boxes of handbags and shoes her mother went through seasonally and Ava had offered to help her. She didn't know who else to tell.

Ava drummed her fingers on the steering wheel. "He was busy cooking and I felt like teasing him so I said, 'So when do we get married?' I didn't think he'd take me seriously."

"This is Dai we're talking about. He couldn't spot sarcasm if it came in the form on an anvil and fell on his head."

"I know. I have to fix this somehow. He's already bought me a ring." She chose not to tell her sister that he'd arranged for a jeweler to come to the house with two cases filled with of an assortment of rings for her to choose from. She didn't want to guess how much that had cost him. Dai did few things by halves. "He also gave me keys to his place and wants to shop for new bedding and... It's not funny."

"Of course it is. You know how he feels about you. He'd repaint his house if you told him it'd make you happy."

"I didn't think—"

"Stop thinking. You've spent so long fooling others you've started fooling yourself."

"What?"

"You weren't really teasing him. You want to marry him but you're too chicken to admit it."

"I want to marry him?"

"Yes."

Ava stared at the road ahead. It was strange. She rarely thought about what she wanted. She always considered what others wanted, how her actions would impact them. But did she want to marry Dai?

She hadn't been sure she wanted to stay in her chosen career, she wasn't sure of the friends she'd selected to spend time with.

But being with Dai for the rest of her life she felt certain of. As much as it terrified her.

"Yes, I do want to marry him. You're right."

"Of course I am."

She stopped at a traffic light and leaned over and kissed Cat on the cheek. "Maybe you can come live with us." She didn't like the thought of Cat being the only one remaining at home even though it was expected that she'd care for their parents in their latter years. Few saw much prospect for her. Her life was the most tied to theirs.

"Why?" Cat said with a laugh. "So I can be a default nanny? No thank you."

She couldn't tell if her sister was really happy and resigned with the future planned for her or not. She never talked about leaving. Or staying for that matter. For a second Ava wasn't sure she knew her sister very well at all. "No, I'm serious. If you want to leave—"

Cat squeezed her hand. "I'll be alright. I'm more worried about you."

Ava watched the light turn green and put her foot on the gas. "Why?"

Cat lowered the window, closed her eyes and let the breeze hit her face. "Because you still have one little problem."

"What is it?"

Cat opened one eye and studied her for a second before she closed it again and leaned her head back. "Mom is going to kill you."

41

———

THE DAY of reckoning came sooner than expected. Ava had overslept and was rushing to her office with a half eaten bagel in her mouth, knowing she had fifteen minutes before her first client arrived when her office manager stopped her in the hallway.

Ava took the bagel from her mouth. "Um, there's been a change in—"

"It's okay," Ava reassured the sandy haired man. It wasn't like Neil to look so out of sorts. "Whoever you had to shuffle around is fine."

"It's not like that," Neil said hurrying behind her. "I couldn't stop her from going into your office. She was very insistent."

Ava inwardly groaned. She knew Ms. Carlow could be bossy when it came to her daughter's appointments.

"It's okay."

"But—"

Ava took out her cell phone. It had been buzzing nonstop

since she'd arrived at the office, but she hadn't had a chance to look at it.

She glanced and saw a bunch of texts from Cat. What on earth?

Ava opened the door to her office and finally understood.

She met the predatory eyes of a leopard dressed in a tailored suit when her mother turned to face her.

"I'll get you some tea," Neil said then left.

Ava walked in and closed the door. She placed the bagel on the desk.

"This is a surprise."

She'd decorated her office to be friendly and cozy for kids and teens. They would walk into a room with blue walls and the pop of orange and yellow colored chairs, stuffed animals and toys, but her mother's presence dimmed the usual brightness of the room. Ava half-expected one of the robots left on the ground to come to life and attack her.

The fact that the sun was shining helped, although the way it touched the silver buckle on her mother's shoes made it shine with the same ominous glint of a knife blade.

"No more lies. You did not go on a business trip."

Ava sat behind her desk. "How do you know that?"

"I had you followed. You should know better than to try and keeps secrets from me. I know that you've been spending time at that man's house."

"That man's name is Dai."

"Why did you lie? Why did you—"

She stopped when Neil knocked on the door and entered with the tea tray. Once he'd gone her mother continued.

"Why are you doing this to me? What has gone wrong?"

"Nothing," she said silently kicking herself. Of course her mother would have her followed. She shouldn't have underestimated her.

"You will come home immediately and we will discuss—"

"I'm going to marry him."

Mrs. Kayode sipped her tea.

"Mom, did you hear me?"

She carefully set the tea cup down. "I recently met a man from England his parents are from Mali."

"Mom, I am marrying Dai."

"He's very well-mannered—"

"Mom!"

"Don't you raise your voice at me," she demanded in a low voice.

"I need you to listen. Please."

"I will no longer stand for this needless rebellion. Dai is not—"

"Marrying you. He is marrying me. I don't care what you think of him. He's one of the finest men I know and I am going to marry him."

"Then you will be miserable. You won't be able to take that child of his to any events. You'll be isolated. And left to care for a child whose own mother doesn't want him."

"I want him. I love Donovan."

"That man is damaged goods. He couldn't manage one marriage who's to say he'll do better with another."

"Who's Maya's father?"

Her mother gasped, stared at her dumbfounded. Slowly her lips thinned and her eyes turned to onyx as a chilled silence filled the room.

Ava clasped her hands together. She knew she'd gone too far and yet it still didn't feel far enough. Her mother held secrets, her mother wasn't all that she seemed. For a moment Ava saw a reflection of herself. Someone who lived a lie when it suited her.

Her mother lifted her tea cup. "I'm waiting for an apology."

Ava sighed. "I'm sorry."

A pleased look briefly touched her face. "Sorry enough to make things right?"

Ava felt the fissures of fear and fought to bank them down. Her mother could cut her out of her life just as she had Maya. A part of her did want to still please her, that part that still took solace in her praise.

But another part screamed out for freedom. Freedom to live and love as herself.

Completely herself with no secrets.

"Your father didn't marry me out of pity."

"I didn't mean—"

"You know nothing about me," her mother said. "What I've had to go through so that you can achieve all that you have. You are throwing away all the sacrifices I've made.

"You were too good. Too perfect." She stood. "I should have known you'd eventually disappoint me."

Her words pierced Ava like an ice pick. She felt the tears build but refused to let them fall.

Wordlessly, she watched her mother walk out the door.

Ava made it through the rest of the day on autopilot then drove to Dai's house, glad she'd gotten there before he had, and walked upstairs then collapsed on the bed. She felt spent but was too tired to sleep.

But she must have drifted off because she hadn't heard him come home and didn't realize he was there until she felt the bed shift.

She felt the warm touch of his hand against her face, smelled cinnamon and sugar, and heard the tender note in his voice when he said, "Are you okay?"

"My mom knows about us now."

"You've been crying."

She closed her eyes. "Off and on."

She heard him sigh in frustration, then the tapping of his hand against the bed sheets. "What can I do?"

"You don't have to do anything."

"It's time for me to talk to her."

She opened her eyes and grabbed his hand before he could stand. "Not yet."

"I can win her over. I hate how miserable she makes you because of me."

Ava shook her head. "No, not because of you. You're just an excuse." She sat up and hugged him. "She's disappointed that I'm not the daughter she wants me to be."

He held her tight. "I don't want you to regret marrying me. I don't want it to cost you your family."

She didn't want to think about the loss of her mother's affection or her father's approval. The thought tore at her heart. She took a deep breath, inhaling his scent, gaining courage by his solid embrace. "I'll still have my sisters and you'll be my family. I think it's a fair exchange." She drew back and looked at him, suddenly wary. "Now we have to tell Donovan."

Dai grinned, unconcerned. "He won't be a problem. I'm sure he'll be thrilled."

42

———————

But when Donovan returned from Jamaica and they sat him down in the living room and told him, his eyes filled with tears.

His gaze shifted between them. "You're getting married?"

Dai nodded.

"To each other?"

"Yes," Dai said confused by his son's reaction. He'd thought Donovan would be jumping around with joy not looking heartbroken.

"But you can't."

"Why not?"

"Because I was going to marry her first."

Dai laughed. "You're too young, Dynamo."

Donovan gripped his hands into fists, his voice tight with anger. "I know that. I was going to wait until I was older."

"Well now you get to live with Sandy and don't have to wait."

"It's not the same."

"Of course it's not the same," Dai said, trying to sound

understanding rather than amused. "She'll be your stepmother. Wouldn't you like that?"

"No, no I wouldn't! You can't marry her." He raced out of the room.

Ava and Dai looked at each other perplexed.

Dai spoke first. "I don't know what to say. Most times I don't know what's going on in his mind but this..." He shook his head. "I knew he loved you but I never thought he saw me as a rival."

"I'm not sure it's that," Ava said slowly. "I think there's something else. This is important..." She nudged him with her elbow, he started to laugh. "It's not funny."

"Yes, it is."

"No, it's not. I won't marry you if he doesn't want me to."

His amusement swiftly died. "You don't mean that."

"How can I marry you when he feels like this? You two come as a pair."

"He's a kid with a crush. He'll get over it."

"You have to go and talk to him."

"And tell my seven year old son about the birds and the bees?"

"No need. We've already had that talk when he was five."

Dai stared at her stunned. "You didn't."

"I had to. We'd been watching an animal show and then there were these two turtles—"

Dai held up his hand. "I don't want to know."

She pinched his cheek amused by his embarrassment. "You're adorable."

He pushed her hand away. "Shut up."

"Go and talk to him."

Dai reluctantly stood. He was going to marry Ava and he wasn't going to let a pint sized tornado get in his way no matter how much he loved him. "Okay. But if I can't convince him we'll give him time to get used to the idea. Just don't say that again."

"What?"

"That you won't marry me."

She stared at him for a moment then her face softened as if she realized how much her words had hurt him. "Alright. I'm sorry, we'll get through this together."

He nodded, the feeling of unease dissipating. "Hmm."

Ava stood up and pushed him towards the stairs. "But right now you're on your own."

DAI TOOK a deep breath before he entered his son's room. He found Donovan sitting in the corner facing the wall. Other children might find that a punishment but for some reason it always gave his son comfort as he alternated between tapping one side then the other in a rhythmic motion.

"Tell me what's going on, Dynamo."

He continued tapping.

"Don't you want Sandy to live with us?"

The tapping increased.

"You're making her feel bad. Should I tell her to go home?"

"No." Donovan pounded the wall then jumped to his feet, dove onto the bed, buried his face in the pillows and started to cry.

Dai blinked, finally realizing how truly upset his son was. He didn't know where to begin. He knew he was big for seven but he never dreamed he'd feel like this. "Sandy...is a lot older than you are."

"I know, I know, I know," Donovan said each word filled with misery.

Dai sat on the edge of the bed. "Remember she was going to marry someone else."

Donovan lifted his head and wiped his eyes. "Yes, can't she marry someone else?"

His son looked so hopeful that it hurt. "Why don't you want her to marry me?"

"Because if you divorce her I'll never see her again."

Dai sighed. Divorce. Of course. Why hadn't he thought of that? His divorce had changed both their lives.

He cleared his throat and chose his words carefully. "Divorce doesn't mean you never get to see someone again. It's meant for when two people can't live together anymore."

"Can't you just stay friends? Can't it be like this forever?"

"No, because I love her and I want to marry her."

His lip trembled. "You'll fight about me and then she'll disappear and never want to see me." He buried his face in the pillows again.

Dai lightly stroked his back.

"We didn't get divorced because of you. Your mother...You know your mother loves you. She's busy that's why you don't see her as much because she's...it's not because of divorce," he finished lamely. He hated lying.

"I don't want Sandy to go away."

"She's not going anywhere. We're not going to get a divorce. But if we did, she'd still see you. I'd make sure of that and she would too."

Donovan sat up and glared at him. "If you divorce her I'll hate you for the rest of my life."

Spoken with the true passion of a child. But he wouldn't make fun.

"I'm not going to divorce her. I love her."

"Did you love Mom when you married her?"

"Yes. Sometimes love changes. But the way I love Sandy..."

He couldn't put it into words. He was at a loss on how to express himself. "I love her very much," he finally said.

"Do you love her more than me?"

"Not more but different. You'll understand when you're older."

"Does Sandy love you more than me?"

Dai paused, feeling completely out of his depth. He wished Ava was in his place since she was better at answering his son's rapid fire questions than he was. "No," he finally said, feeling certain of his words as he remembered the look on Ava's face when she'd first held Donovan as a baby. "She's loved you your entire life."

Donovan grinned relieved. "Really?"

"Yes, really."

"I've loved her my whole life too."

"I know you have. I think you should go downstairs and tell her that. I think you hurt her feelings."

Donovan's eyes widened with fear. "I didn't mean to do that. Did I make her cry?"

"No. but you can make things better."

"How?"

"Tell her what you told me and you'll be fine."

Donovan jumped out of bed and raced out of the room. Dai sighed and hung his head. He knew it was just the opinions of a child but it still hurt that his son thought he'd mess things up with Ava. God he hoped not. She meant too much to him. But what if...

He thought of the demise of his marriage, all the things he could have done to save it and all the things he couldn't have done. He faced the reality that despite all of his wealth, he couldn't buy his way into the same league as his ex-wife. His ex knew it.

So did Ava. Soon Dai's mind filled with all the reasons

Ava's mother didn't think he was worthy of her daughter. He still had so much more to prove.

He looked up when he heard soft footsteps. He noticed his son peeking his head in the door way. "What is it?"

Donovan shuffled into the room, avoiding his gaze. "Dad, I'm sorry. I don't want you to be sad."

"Sad?"

He looked at him. "That Sandy loves me more." He tugged on the hem of his T-shirt. "I'm glad you're marrying Sandy so that no one else can have her."

Dai held out his arm and Donovan ran to him, allowing Dai to embrace him in a fierce hug. "Thanks, Dynamo. I needed to hear that."

AVA ACCEPTED Donovan's heartfelt apology and they all worked on becoming a family. She moved into their house and Donovan started a new school year.

Promise was in the air.

Ava felt triumphant. She'd fought for what was important to her and won.

But that October she'd discover that while facing her mother had been terrifying, the worst was yet to come.

43

"WE NEED TO TALK," Dai said his cool tone belied the fire in his eyes.

Ava blinked at him as she faced him in the foyer.

After a tiring day, the last thing she expected to be met with was a face that looked like thunder.

He turned.

"What's going on?" she asked, stumbling after him as she quickly removing her shoes.

"You tell me." He walked into the living room and pointed to the sofa. She sat and he pushed up the sleeves of his sweater before he began to pace. "I spoke to another parent at Donovan's school about their trip to the junkyard. To my surprise there wasn't a trip to the junkyard. It never happened." He stopped in front of her and folded his arms. "So how did my son end up in a junkyard?"

Ava opened her mouth, a ready lie on her lip, but it died when Dai pinned her with a dark look and said, "Careful what you say."

She sighed in defeat. "Remember when I told you he took the bus to the end of the line?"

Dai nodded.

"Well, he didn't explore the bus depot. He went across the street and walked around the junkyard. The manager called me after they'd discovered him pretending to drive an old Cadillac. That's where I picked him up."

He fell quiet a moment then said, "So you lied to me."

"Let me explain."

"Explain what?" he shouted, his arms falling to his sides. "Why you lied to me twice?! Twice, Ava."

"D-dai—" Ava said, stumbling over his name, shaken by his anger but knowing she deserved it.

He lowered his voice, his dark gaze bore into her. "I asked you specifically to tell me what happened. And you lied the day it happened and then again when you told me it was a school trip. You looked straight at me and lied to my face. To. My. Face, Ava!"

Ava lowered her gaze, wracked with guilt and shame. "Dai, I—"

"And if that wasn't bad enough, you had Donovan lie to me too." He laughed without humor. "Must have been real funny for the both of you keeping this from me."

Ava rubbed her hands together and shook her head. "No, that's not—"

Dai shook his head. "I'm used to my ex breaking her promises but I expect better from you, Ava."

She looked up at him. "I was trying to protect you."

Those words enraged him more. His eyes blazed with anger. "Protect me from what? The truth?" He tapped his chest. "I'm his father! I needed to know. You don't keep secrets like that from me. But more than that, you don't lie to me." He pointed at her.

"You know..." He squeezed his eyes shut, fighting to take control of his anger. "Because of my father..." He took a deep breath and glared at her. "You of all people *know* how much trust means to me. How much it hurts when people lie to me and yet you still —" He turned away from her unable to finish and paced again.

Ava felt the tears build and hated them. She hated getting in trouble, even more she hated disappointing the people she cared about. Especially him. "You're right. I'm sorry."

Dai shook his head and she knew her words weren't enough.

Her heart trembled at the words he didn't say. *I don't trust you anymore. You're no better than Elena. Than my ex, than my father, than anyone who's ever let me down and hurt me.*

Her greatest fear had come true. He now saw she was a fraud. A true rotten liar.

She lied most of her life. She lied about being happy when she was sad, she shaped herself to be whatever someone else wanted her to be. But she'd never lied to him. Until now.

She'd betrayed him in the worst way. She'd lied about his son. How could he forgive her for this? *I expected better from you.*

She glanced down at the engagement ring on her finger and slowly pulled it off no longer feeling worthy of it. She pressed it between her hands. "I know what I did was wrong, but it seemed innocent enough."

"Innocent? What other innocent things aren't you telling me about my son?"

"It's not like that. Donovan—"

"This isn't about him. It's about you."

Small footsteps pounded into the room.. "I knew it!" Donovan cried. "You're fighting because of me."

"No, we're not," Dai said. "Go to your room."

"You are," Donovan shouted. "You said my name. You're mad at Sandy and it's my fault. You're making her cry."

"No, he's not," Ava said gently, wiping her eyes. "I'm sad because I messed up. You didn't do anything wrong. It's not your fault. It's mine."

"Go to your room," Dai told him.

"But—"

Dai's tone hardened to steel. "I'll give you 'til the count of three."

"No!" Donovan glared at him.

Dai glared back. "One."

Tears spilled down his cheek. "You promised you wouldn't break up."

"Two."

Ava knelt in front of Donovan desperate to calm him and defuse the situation. "I know you're upset but your father has every right to be angry with me. I should have told him the truth about the junkyard."

"But I told you—"

"Yes, but I shouldn't have listened. I'm an adult and I made a mistake. When you do something wrong you face up to it. And that's what I'm doing now."

"But Sandy—"

"Your father deserves respect. You must listen to him."

Donovan trembled with anger. He glanced down and noticed the engagement ring gone from her hand. "But he's sending you away."

Dai made a sound of surprise.

Ava spoke before he could say anything. "I promise I won't leave without seeing you first. Now go to your room as your father asked."

Donovan sent an angry glance at his father and said,

"Remember your promise," before he spun away and ran out of the room.

A tense silence descended.

Ava placed the engagement ring on the coffee table with a soft click. "I should go. I'll—"

Dai didn't look at her. "How come it's so easy for you?"

"What?"

"It's so easy for you to walk away. It was easy for her too," he said referring to his ex. "Leave, I won't stop you."

Ava blinked. He sounded more resigned and hurt than angry.

"I don't have the strength tonight, but I'll do it tomorrow. For now I'll sleep on the couch."

Dai spun around and faced her. "What are you talking about?"

"Moving my things out."

He frowned. "Why would you do that?"

Her heart constricted. He didn't even want her in the house anymore? Was it really over? Did he really want her gone? She couldn't imagine going back home, she could stay with Maya and Keeden but she really didn't want to leave. Dai and Donovan were her home now. She would fight to stay and until she got him to forgive her. She swallowed. "You won't have to see me. I'll stay out of your way and—"

Dai waved his hand. "You're not making any sense."

What didn't he understand? Sometimes he could be so dense. She spoke slowly. "I'm moving out of your bedroom—"

"Why would I want that?" he snapped.

"Because..." He wasn't making any sense. "I-I thought... Isn't this what you wanted?"

"Did I say that?"

"No, but you're so angry with me."

"Yes. Very."

"And you shouted at me."

"Yes! Because that's what I do, Ava. You know that. I have a temper. I sometimes swear. I'll punch things."

She surged to her feet propelled by an anger of her own. "But I don't want to make you angry. I don't want to disappoint you. I can't bear the thought of letting you down. I don't want you to shout at me like Mom shouts at Maya or how you shout at your ex. I don't want to be that person who causes you pain."

Dai shook his head, the fire in his eyes ebbing. "Ava, it's not the same."

"It is. I hurt you. You're right I should have known better. I betrayed you and I taught your son a terrible lesson. So I'll work harder to deserve you."

"Deserve me?" his voice cracked in surprise.

"Yes." Ava picked up the ring, walked around the coffee table and stood in front of him. She took a deep breath, gathering her courage before she got down on one knee then the other.

This time the act wasn't a strategic move or a dramatic display. This time every action was real. She kept her head lowered and quietly said, "I'm ashamed of myself." Her voice shook, a new anguish piercing her heart. "I'm not always nice or good or sweet. I can lie and be deceitful and vengeful and a little selfish. You are so good. So much better than I am. Kinder, sweeter." She placed the ring in her hands and lifted them up to him. "But I don't want to lose you. I'll work hard to change and become—"

Dai snatched the ring and lifted her to her feet. "Stop that."

Ava blinked at him startled. He seemed even angrier than before. Why wouldn't he let her apologize? "But—"

"I don't need you to change," he said. He swore and shook his head exasperated. "Auntie's right. You really are clueless sometimes." He took her hand. "Just because I get mad at you," he slid the ring back on her finger, "doesn't mean I've stopped loving you."

She hadn't lost him? He'd forgiven her already? She hadn't permanently disappointed him? He could still look at her that way?

Ava hung her head and cried in relief.

Dai pulled her close, held her tight and affectionately said, "You dummy."

She cupped his face and kissed him, her heart buoyant with joy. "I love you so much."

"About time you figured that out."

She laughed and took his hand. "Let's go."

His eyes heated with desire. "I thought you said you were tired."

Ava playfully punched him. "Not that. We have to talk to Donovan."

Dai swore. "You're right. I'm not sure I handled that well. I don't know what to say."

"That's okay." She led him to the stairs. "I know what to do."

Donovan lifted his head from his pillow and turned when he heard something at his bedroom door.

Through a hazy film of tears he saw his dad and Sandy standing in the doorway.

They were holding hands.

He wiped his eyes.

Dad didn't look angry and Ava didn't look sad. He cautiously sat up.

"It's okay," Ava said.

His father motioned him forward.

He climbed out of bed and shuffled over to him still unsure whether he was in trouble.

His father lifted him up in his arms and hugged him tight. "We'll talk about your junkyard adventure later," he whispered.

Donovan hugged him back, glad it wouldn't be tonight, glad that his dad sounded happy. He pulled back and turned to Sandy. She looked happy too. He reached out his arm towards her and she stepped closer, letting him hug her too while she hugged him back.

Donovan released a contented sigh, feeling a rare sense of calm as he settled into the warmth of their embrace, their acceptance, their love.

EPILOGUE

AVA LOOKED over the paperwork on her desk as a light summer rain tapped against her office window. She'd so enjoyed her work at Boulders and Bridges she and Alexis had decided to collaborate on a community project that would help expand the program throughout the school year.

She turned a page and jotted some ideas her brother-in-law, Bryant, had given her, then glanced at the picture of Donovan and Dai framed on her desk. Donovan was proudly grinning and sporting a peace sign in front of a lopsided volcano structure while his serious looking father tried to fix it.

To her relief the energetic eight year old hadn't caused any havoc at their wedding, which they'd hosted in Dai's backyard and resembled more of a small family barbecue than wedding ceremony.

Her parents were less than impressed.

Fortunately, their twenty guests enjoyed themselves too much to notice.

Dai's mother had an animated discussion with Maya and Keeden; Dai's cousin Koji and his girlfriend Moriko patiently entertained Gwen while she listed all the possible names she and her husband had received for the baby they were expecting next year.

Cat kept Donovan and Auntie entertained with skillful impressions of her parents without the objects of her amusement noticing.

But the biggest surprise was how much her mother changed when Dai's father arrived.

The pinched face beauty quickly fell for the handsome, wealthy and charming flatterer. Laughing prettily at everything he said and demurely accepting his praise for raising such fine daughters.

Soon she couldn't speak of Dai highly enough. She gushed about all his accomplishments and excellent pedigree.

The memory of her mother's change of heart still amused her.

Ava glanced up when someone knocked on the door. "Come in."

Dai sauntered in. "I've come to treat you to lunch." He held up his hand. "I checked your schedule so I know you have time."

"I wasn't going to say no."

Her cell phone rang just as she was about to stand. She frowned at the unfamiliar number. "Hello?"

"Are you Donovan Lartey's mother?"

She glanced at Dai then cautiously said, "Yes."

"I'm a nurse at Renton General Hospital. Your son's fine and the burns are minor but you should get here as soon as you can."

"Okay." Ava disconnected and quickly grabbed her handbag.

Dai looked at her curious. "What was that about?"

She sent him a look and his shoulders sagged. "Donovan?"

"Donovan."

"I'll go."

"No, it's okay. Like you said, I have the time."

Dai held the door open for her. "I swear that kid is attracted to Trouble."

Ava laughed and agreed.

Until they had their daughter Lily.

ABOUT THE AUTHOR

Dara Girard, an award-winning, national bestselling author of more than fifty novels, from romance to suspense, loves telling stories.

Born in the US to immigrant parents, Dara enjoys pulling from her Jamaican, British, Nigerian heritage and exposure to various cultures to bring what reviewers and fans call "vivid emotional stories" to life. She is best known for her popular Henson Series, the mysterious Clifton Sisters, and the fun Black Stockings Society.

You can write her at:
contactdara@daragirard.com
or
ILORI Press Books
c/o Dara Girard
P.O. Box 10332
Silver Spring, MD 20914
If you'd like to receive a reply, please send a self-addressed stamped envelope.

Visit her website to sign up for her newsletter and get sneak peeks, monthly updates on new releases, and special offers.

For more information visit
www.daragirard.com

www.ingramcontent.com/pod-product-compliance
Lightning Source LLC
Chambersburg PA
CBHW061548210726

48287CB00006B/2118